427 GIL
Gilbert, Erzsebet FEB 2013
Logodaedaly

D1058231

KILGORE MEMORIAL LIBRARY
520 NEBRASKA AVE.
YORK, NE 68467

PRAISE FOR
Logodædaly

"Ms. Gilbert's *Logodædaly* is a feat of writerly derring-do, a Borgesian excursion, one both gleeful and droll. She is a skilled fabulist, an astute lover of the more recondite quarters of the English language, and the reader's charming and witty companion-guide across this erudite terrain."

— Barry Lopez

"In 1951, novelist, logophile and lepidopterist Vladimir Nabokov shed his cloak of European elan and pulled on hiking boots to tramp Colorado's mountains in search of rare butterflies. Sixty years later, he has returned! But this time it's in the spirit and intellect of young but worldly and word-drunk Erzsébet Gilbert, a fellow gourmand of the wonderful, whose shimmering tales would have delighted him. Actually, this book will delight anyone."

—John Calderazzo, author of
Rising Fire: Volcanoes & Our Inner Lives

"Erzsébet Gilbert has brought an entire hidden lexicon of the imagination to life by reincarnating words into the forms of their lost meanings. The writer's enchantment comes through in every syllable that appears bewitchingly on these pages. As a bibliotaph myself, I loved every moment I spent with this peerless volume of wonder."

—Rita J. King, author of
Big Easy Money: Disaster Profiteering on the American Gulf Coast
and director of Dancing Ink Productions

"The scope of Erzsébet Gilbert's *Logodædaly* is beautiful, transfixing, and magical. It's as if inebriated on dreams, Samuel Johnson woke up in the forest and began his dictionary project with not just words in mind, but set out also to define fauna, curiosities, legends, nonexistent cities, and the whole of the incorporeal world. Gilbert's florid imagination and lore-like prose will sweep you into a lush lexical wonderland."

—Evan P. Schneider, author of *A Simple Machine, Like the Lever*

"Opening this book is thrilling, something like getting a box of chocolates with no guide to what's inside them. Verbal effervescence of this caliber is a rare treat. Highly recommended."

—*ForeWord Reviews*

"A gourmet spread of bizarre, wacky, and magical words that you've never uttered and probably never will....but what fun to watch how audaciously Erzsébet has played, flirted, danced, and juggled their sounds and meanings. Following a complex pronunciation guide and a brief definition of each word, Gilbert frivolously weaves them into amusing period tales and scenes from centuries past. They're perfect snacks to munch when you're looking for linguistic nourishment."

—Rita Golden Gelman, author of *Tales of a Female Nomad, Living at Large in the World* and more than 70 children's books

LOGODÆDALY,

OR, SLEIGHT-OF-WORDS

*Being a compendium of very old words,
or those little-used,
and other artifacts
of the English language,
and many Wondrous Things,
in a new edition
now with pictures,
and sundry stories
conjured, or stolen,
and suitably transformed,
which the Discerning Reader might find useful
in conversation or in Love;
a dictionary.*

Erzsébet Gilbert

Illustrated by Sherise Talbott

WOLVERINE FARM PUBLISHING
FORT COLLINS, COLORADO

WOLVERINE FARM PUBLISHING is a 50I(c)3 nonprofit organized for literary, educational, scientific, and charitable purposes. To learn more about our organization, please visit www.wolverinefarm.org.

Text copyright © 2011 Erzsébet Gilbert
Illustrations © 2011 Sherise Talbott

No part of this book may be used or reproduced
in any manner whatsoever without written permission of the publisher.

Parts of this book are works of fiction, and any resemblance to actual persons,
living or dead, is purely coincidental.

For more information please address:
Wolverine Farm Publishing, PO BOX 814,
Fort Collins, CO 80522

FIRST EDITION
14 13 12 11   6 5 4 3 2 1

Printed and bound in The United States of America on recycled paper
according to industry standards established by the Green Press Initiative.

ISBN: 978-0-9823372-9-5

For David,
who forever transforms
the meaning of
love

That which may be found lurking within this Book, or, a Table of its Contents

Acknowledgements from the Author, who cannot find words enough to express gratitude

Even when absentminded and prone to distraction by shimmering objects, the author forever and inexpressibly must thank those without whose genius, creativity, and care this Book would have never appeared:

to Todd Simmons and Megan Schiel, for not only their invaluable editorial input, but for their fond wisdom, genuine heart, and unflagging friendship, and
to Sherise Talbott, for her elfin spirit and the otherworld of her art, and
to Abigail Yeagle, for her enthusiasm and vital help, and
to Rita J. King, for her earnest reading and for her sparkling character,
to John Calderazzo, for his reading and his adept mentorship amidst writing and vulcanism, and
to Evan P Schneider, for reading this work, and unveiling his own literary creation in happy exchange, and
to Paul Trembath, for overturning the way I think about language in every single utterance,
to Simon Winchester, for his correspondence, and for his brilliant research of English and the world, and
to a century's worth of contributors to the *Oxford English Dictionary,* whose unrelenting labors and loves created that epical lexicon, and to the editors of Oxford University Press for their continuing work, and
to Emily Bailey and Arianna Prothero, for a childhood of true faerie stories in the willow trees, and

to my family, always: to Mom, for the libraries and the glitter we pasted in matchbooks, and for reading to me in the rocking chair when I'm sleepy, and

in memory, to Bob, for so much laughter, love, and blues and the abstract truth, and

to James and Thomas, for learning curse words with me, for the marker scribbled all over your cheeks, and for being my heroes, the bravest people I know, and

to Anyu and Apu, for the gift of an entirely new language and its words to say I love you—*szeretlek, a pompás családom,* and

in memory, to Dad, for giving me the microcosm of the *Oxford English Dictionary* and the macrocosms of the stars, and the sense of wonder which sees beauties defying words, and

to David, for the revivified copy of the dictionary which burnt, and for your unending support, adventures, illuminations, and love.

An author's note, or, how this Book Happened-to-Be

Much in the manner of one of those obscure storybook sorcerers whose papery touch upon the palm either divines or directs history, it was the *Oxford English Dictionary* which proved responsible for this book, in addition to my own experiences of explosive fires, neurosurgery, and true love. As etymology amounts to the chronicle of a word's multifarious lifetime (and one ought never trust the autobiography of the word itself, for they are liars, thieves, and lunatics all), one understands that the Book (and mayhap I myself) possesses such a traceable history, a narrative I clutch strangely near to my fading, flawed, valiant heart.

I can recall the enchantment of my manic childhood fingers upon the embossed insignia of the complete *Oxford English Dictionary* that once rested solemnly amongst the mathematic tomes of my father's study. There are the arcane murmurings of the miniscule type—so small that in a squint the characters grow arachnid, spinning away on widowed or venomous feet to leave a thread of gossamer I swear I can discern upon the page. Such heightened perception emerges, of course, from the spooky magnifying glass which accompanies the dictionary as a sentinel, so that in reading the tiny print one will not go blind or accidentally disappear. In words I possessed

9

the wanton freedoms and fears which forever come with incomprehension, and with each story my tender mother read to me, the perilous idea that I myself might one day write a tale as Real Writers do. My first spoken word— to this day still a lump of sugar waxing round within the mouth—was *moon*; the first I found myself elated to read aloud was *bump* (which I suppose one might consider some sort of omen, if in a soothsaying state of mind).

And older, slightly taller, with my vocabulary augmented to include multiple synonyms for blue and some quite filthy curses, I indulged in the unpardonably nerdy process of browsing the dictionary: its endless intrigue and memoriams, thrilling shards of definition and the sainthood of paper cuts. A twinkle of chance, and thence the most striking and sweet of my finds: *melliferous*, that is, "producing or yielding honey." Reading this at one o'clock in the morning, I surrendered to a feverish and insomniac need to write a story by that name. One is at times surprised to discover the odd characters sailing and singing scat within one's mind, which is not to say I had been entirely unaware of my own alternate selves, but those were mostly used to pardon errors such as broken plates or minor theft.

A twinkle of chance, and in a rather manic mood I submitted *Melliferous* to a writing contest, about which I promptly forgot—until a particular telephone call summoned me to the office of Wolverine Farm Publishing. Hello, I said, more effusive than type communicates— while inwardly I blinked at the most luminescent of people

I had ever encountered: blinding with the good-graced hands of a writer and the remembered adventures of a wanderer's eye, a redefinition of the human pulse. In much the manner of a comedy or a novel of mystery (either perhaps involving bowler hats), 'twas a case of mistaken identity, as I believed said person to be Todd Simmons, head of Wolverine Farm Publishing. The one with whom I was quietly and helplessly enamored was my love, David Rozgonyi, their fiction editor, though at the first electrical touch of our two hands I could think it to be no more than a melliferous dream. I had in fact won the aforementioned contest (the award money instantly squandered upon arcane books), leading to creative collaboration and profound friendship, and a love for which I as writer and speaker and organism lacked words.

Outside the thoroughly enjoyable and pragmatically useless process of studying writing and the philosophy of science in hectic university halls, and the tumult of falling in love (O! *moon* in the heart!), I began editorial work at Wolverine Farm's literary journal, *Matter*. Nonetheless and nevertheless, I simultaneously continued the idle practice of extracting dainties out of the OED and writing for each a little anecdote. A standard recreational pursuit for those trendsetters in the know, right?

But as circumstances are wont to take their somersaults, in due course I awoke in a pale room under that unnatural scent of constant sanitation, with nausea and staples in my head, whereupon I unhesitatingly murmured *yes* to David's wedding proposal as he stood perpetually by my bed (and then, as a most romantic side effect of anesthesia, I vomited). As I was informed and believed not, I and my beloved brothers had been in an automotive accident and lay now in a hospital's care. Apparently, we were briefly on fire, and truly quite overdramatically my head had split open and required two surgeries; 'twould seem that nine days of amnesia had been compassionate, lending me disbelieving shimmers rather than trauma. O! the *bump* upon the head!

But in blood, ink, and ash—the fundamental elements, according to some—the invaluable old copy of the OED given that day to me by my devoted father had burnt somewhere upon a riverside road, the whispering death of definitions. And I think it not excessive to conjecture now that the added weight of all those words may have influenced for good or ill the acrobatic automobile. I may blame the page, if I am feeling irresponsible today. I may thank the page, as well, for I remain alive to read and write and breathe. I myself was left with double vision, faulty depth perception, and a scar in the form of a question-mark, which if in a literary mood one may read as accidental metaphors.

Apart from subsequently acquiring green eyeglasses, a lapis ring, and a fresh copy of the dictionary given unto me by David, in the year to come I amassed also some one hundred diminutive tales regarding English words—at which point the notion of publication began to take form. As since those days of running grubby fingers over the OED I had dreamt of the peril of being a Real

Writer, I leapt with awkward feline voracity at the idea, soon discovering its sheer fun, a number of symbols of pronunciation, and a large vocabulary of frivolity. And following my transcontinental emigration to Hungary, a nation of a decidedly complicated, non-Indo-European tongue, and after the little frustrations of print and the virtuosity of illustration, thus came this day—here, Dear Reader, as surely you have noticed, with the asymmetric weight of the Book unfurled in your two hands like a bruising butterfly.

The Author is quite happy, it must be said. Indeed, never might she have predicted the improbable consequences of the language, had she been asked in simple childish vocabulary in the dusty and susurrating study, years ago. But it is the artifice, the deviousness, the thrall of words which brought me to this. From *moon* and *bump* and *melliferous* unto a small story of love, cranial surgery, and the printed page. But, then again, perhaps this is one of the language's inevitable implications. For while the elusive and allusive and illusive characters of any given alphabet configure and reconfigure and conspire into words with which we momentarily remake the precious world, words we pretend we might comprehend and which might possess some actual meaning that can endure—thus does the too-brief existence of any given word represent forever a plenum of possible tales, those that have truly scarred and transformed us and those which have not yet come to pass, but forever might potentially occur.

Interesting Questions which may be answered in this Volume:

~ In the fury of the Great Avian Wars, what particular genus of birds was most feared of all?

~ What is the best sort of hat?

~ What disturbing tendencies represent the first signs that one's child is maniac for the feline world?

~ Of what two sorts of porridges might the universe be composed?

~ Who governs the pharaohs' ancient and crumbling tombs? Why is it amused?

~ Of all citizens and pets, who dared climb the endless spiral stair of the city of Ememeer?

~ What was to be the fate of the Lady Eugenia?

~ From what organisms might one learn to become motatorious?

~ In what pursuit might one possibly need to use the word 'suint'?

~ What is your favorite opsony?

~ With what word might one give a lover the promise of anything at all?

~ In the realm of the clouds, what determines the extent to which something is actually real? Are you?

~ What, ultimately, is 'morbidezza'? Explain in three words or less.

~ Where does the Assassin hide, and how at last shall she find the King?

~ In ages to come, what will happen to the waves upon the sea?

~ What lay at the bottom of Eveline's well?

~ How might one recognize the true descendants of the porphyrogenites' royal dynasty?

~ Who is the superior magician: Archibald, or Theodoric?

15

~ *Who spies upon you from beneath the ground?*
~ *In the language of the fan, what is the meaning of a flick of the wrist?*
~ *Where can the exhausted traveler at last find absolute luxury?*
~ *What item was found within the belly of a great fish pulled from the depths of the Adriatic Sea?*
~ *Why do you experience your sudden moments of fremitus?*
~ *Which beastie can manipulate the threads of space and time?*
~ *What do people do upon the moon?*
~ *What shall I name my cat?*

How the Most Honorable Reader, upon opening this book, may utilize its many Anecdotes, Morsels, and Particular Things:

In a manner being somewhat Scampish and Kin of Thievery, this Book has pilfered its Approximate Form from the *Oxford English Dictionary*: thusly, the Reader begins with the *Word* In Question.

logodædaly

At this juncture, the Reader learns how the Word looks most pleasingly spelled, or at least how Scribes find it prettiest. Such an elegant or many-limbed or mildly freakish Word is followed by its *Pronunciation*, that is, when given Blood and Breath and spoken in the mouth. Sundry symbols of English pronunciation (those used within this book) are explained as follows:

The Consonants
b, d, f, k, l, m, n, p, t, v, z remain the same.

g   as in *go, goblin*
dʒ   as in *ledge, soldier, fudge*
ŋ   as in *singing, ding*

ŋg   as in *finger*
ð   as in *then, bathe, blather*
θ   as in *thick, path, thimbleful*
ʒ   as in *vision, treasure*
ʃ   as in *fish, shortcake*
tʃ   as in *chin, chill, witchcraft*
j   as in *yes, beauty, yonder*
w   as in *west, windfall*
hw   as in *when, whee, wheelbarrow*
s   as in *see, distress*
h   as in *hoot, harpsichord*
r   as in *rustic, terrier*
(r) as in *her, chatter*
x   as in *loch, frijoles*

The Vowels

ɪ   as in *wit, pincushion*
ɛ   as in *pet, September*
æ   as in *patter, scandal*
ʌ   as in *bump, succulent, cluster*
ɒ   as in *pot, strong, bebop*
(ə) as in *broken, edible*
i   as in *sappy, uproarious*
ʊ   as in *put, room, bushy*
ɔː   as in *born, corncob*
uː   as in *moon, boom, poop*
ɜː   as in *burn, termite*
ɑː   as in *barn, arm, star*
iː   as in *bean, steam*

ɛː   as in *Fahrenheit, fahre*
ə   as in *another, sweeper, cellar*

The Little Dipthongs, &c.

eɪ   as in *bay, stain, faraway*
aɪ   as in *buy, fine, porkpie*
ɔɪ   as in *toy, alloy, soybean*
əʊ   as in *no, aloe, pony*
ɛə   as in *hair, multifarious, bear*
ʊə   as in *tour, amateur*
aʊ   as in *cow, pounce*
ɪə   as in *seer, teardrop, smear*
ɔə   as in *four, boar, carnivore*
aɪə as in *fiery, attire, liar*
aʊə as in *sour, tower*

( ) surrounding a letter indicates its possible
omission, while ' precedes the syllable of primary
stress, and ˌ precedes those of secondary (not-so-
primary) stress.

But everybody knows that nobody *actually* reads such
tedious charts. Nonetheless, for the Meticulous Savant:

logodædaly
(lɒgəʊˈdiːdəlɪ)

Now the Reader shall find the *Morphology* of the Word,
this being How-It-Came-to-Be: its Etymological Roots in
the language of some-aught country or another, whence

come various peoples from whom the Word is stolen, and its Subsequent Form-History in English, changing as it is warped or misspoken, misspelled or perverted by literary whim and crafty talk. Therefore:

> **logodædaly**
> (lɒgəʊ'di:dəlɪ) [adapted late Latin *logodædalia* (Greek λογοδαιδαλία), from *logos*, λόγος, word, reason, or speech; and *daedalus*, δαίδαλος, cunning, or related to Daedalus, mythic architect of the Minoan Labyrinth and creator of the wax wings of Icarus]

Having gleaned several Notable Facts of History and Tongue, the Reader shall discover the Word's *Part of Speech*, whether it is a Verb denoting actions (instance: one writes), or a Noun to be a Thing (spoon, candelabra, imbecile), or an Adjective describing the nature of a Fruit (red), a Philosopher (cantankerous), or a Cat curled in moonlight (luminous), &c. In this way, one will not by Accident appear foolish in elegant conversation and claim one knows 'how to red' and 'can candelabra most delicately across the ballroom floor.' Thus:

> **logodædaly**
> (lɒgəʊ'di:dəlɪ) [adapted late Latin *logodædalia* (Greek λογοδαιδαλία), from *logos*, λόγος, word, reason, or speech; and *daedalus*,

δαίδαλος, cunning, or related to Daedalus (mythical architect of the Minoan Labyrinth and creator of the wax wings of Icarus)]
NOUN

Now, and about time, appears the *Definition* of the Word, this (purportedly) being its Meaning. A most slippery topic, dear Reader, as with the electriferous sensation of a haunting one realizes that Meaning means Nothing at all (so to speak). That is, *m*, *e*, **A**, **Ω** being no more than the scritch-scratches of the inky quill, and the voice being no more than a few seconds' worth of trembling cords, a definition in present only as it disappears; it can do naught save transform o'er Time and Place and Text and Throat. And Meaning means more than it is, for none may read without the ghoulish burden of hidden undertones, swamped Memory, subtexts which one may or may not know. 'Tis this Full Emptiness which makes the Word matter so much. As in:

logodædaly
(lɒgəʊ'di:dəlɪ) [adapted late Latin *logodædalia* (Greek λογοδαιδαλία), from *logos*, λόγος, word, reason, or speech; and *daedalus*, δαίδαλος, cunning, or related to Daedalus (mythical architect of the Minoan Labyrinth and creator of the wax wings of Icarus)]
NOUN
Cunning in words; skill in adorning a speech; 'verbal legerdemain'.

Yet *if Word, then Story*, or so goes the old proverb in some Far Country whose name we no longer recall. The Word is simply the sign of innumerable Possible Tales. And so it behooves a dictionary to include *Literary Instances*, historically situated Fictions and Facts and Poesies to demonstrate how once the Word may have proved crucial to a tale. Mayhap, dear Reader:

logodædaly
(lɒgəʊˈdiːdəlɪ) [adapted late Latin *lo-godædalia* (Greek *λογοδαιδαλία*), from *logos, λόγος,* word, reason, or speech; and *daedalus, δαίδαλος,* cunning, or related to Daedalus (mythical architect of the Minoan Labyrinth and creator of the wax wings of Icarus)]
NOUN
Cunning in words; skill in adorning a speech; 'verbal legerdemain'.
(**1727** BAILEY. *An universal etymological English Dictionary*) **vol. II** *Logodædaly,* a goodly shew and flourish of words, without much matter; or,
(**2010** GILBERT. *Logodædaly*) **this page** And see also, this book.

The fatally flawed Heroes,
the Villains most sinister,
and the comedic Supporting
Characters of this Book, or,
the Words

abature

(æbətjʊə(r)) [adopted French *abatture*, *abature*, throwing down]
NOUN

The traces left by a stag in a forest's undergrowth through which it has passed.

(1784 S. SHADE ET AL. *The Book of Deer*) p 47 Among other things, cartography has recorded the thousand nebulous nations of the birds, the blue barony of the glaciers, and the not yet existent seas which shall engulf our countries in the centuries to come. What none have yet attempted is a map of the world's abatures. Of course, the deer will scarce surrender unto our censuses or our strict territories, though it would seem indeed that no sooner can a wall be raised before stag is seen vaulting in defiant hyperbola over its locked iron gates. Moreover the forests are feral and thorn-struck and older than we, and e'en from their bulbous balloons the aeronauts can glimpse nothing of the abatures, save for that flash of lustrous motion through the oaks and crying thickets and lachrymose cypresses below; thus are we hindered. Perhaps one might consider a chart of the abatures to be valuable at least to posterity, for it is likely that e'en before we ourselves are swallowed by the waters, the marvelous smoke of our cities shall devour the woods and turn the moss towards grinding

industrial ends, thus obliterating what remains of the deer's flickering paths. Yet in spite of all civilized enterprise, there remain still places upon this globe which for ten thousand sorrowful years have felt not the weight of a human foot, a silent geography of musky silences winding towards the unknown, dappled loci of mating and of mouth, realms whose secret character we cannot fathom—or rather, do not recall.

See also **anachorism, corbin, garguill, urisk**

adelaster

(ædiːˈlæstə(r)) [modern form of Greek ἄδηλος, not manifest + ἄστη, -έρα star] NOUN

A provisional name for a plant whose blooms remain unknown.

(1891 V. L. TESTHEW , ED. *The Arbitrary Flowerbed*) p 7
Arterial are its roots; the leaves murmur nonsense to the gray cadence of the rain and disturb the reels of the honeybees; it sprouts where ink has dripped to fall in faerie rings. Henceforth, as for an adelaster, I shall call it after my love.

See also **corbicula, morbidezza, selenitic, wrancheval**

ætites

(æ'tɪtiːs) [adopted from Latin, *aetītes*, adopted from Greek ἀετίτης, properly from adjective 'of the eagle, aquiline,' substantive 'eagle stone'] NOUN

The eagle-stone; a hollow pebble containing yet another pebble, fabled to be found in an eagle's nest and supposedly capable of detecting theft.

(**1723** A. CORNELIUS & J. T. ATHANASIA. *Treasures to be Catalogued and Possibly Destroyed*) **p 103** Past the penultimate step of the nightmare staircase within Sir Thomas Browne's *Musæum Clausum*, eternally closed and eternally vanished, there

is a chamber where the moonlight be swept up each dawn by the loyal custodial gnomes. Here stands a pedestal which shall burn away the reckless name and brash fingertips of the wretch bold enough to touch it, and upon that pedestal rests the ætites. Some shall claim

that the eagle-stone be as purely empty as are an angel's dreams; others assert that within the ætites there exists yet another hollow pebble within which rattles another hollow pebble and another, on and on and onwards in a geologic rendering of our own universe. What is certain is that one who knows the method of the ætites will possess instantaneously the power to identify a thief with hooded eyes, to recognize the pearls of a stolen crown, to read a falsehood as it flutters blithely through the air. The great irony, however, remains the fact that authenticity is not always freely given, and so that criminal who dares seek the ætites must rob it from the eagles' hidden, covetous, omniscient nests.

See also **gelatia, lygure, naricorn**

ailurophile

(aɪɪl(j)ʊərəʊfaɪl)   [adapted Greek *ailouros*, ἀίλουρος, cat + -*philos*, φίλος, loving or dear] NOUN

A lover of cats.

(**1809** D. PETTIPAT. *Options for the Young Woman: A Handbook for Cultivating One's Suitable Activities, and dodging the inappropriate*) **p 124** Though it shall be admitted that adolescents are so fickle, so prone to the swings and swoops of fashion's chariot and the newest filthy waltzes to glitter through our bright ballrooms, the proper young woman must avoid such corrupting pursuits. They are not, as some would claim, some innocent whimsy, but indeed a disease instantly communicable, like those waterborne animalcules and iniquitous gowns which have immolated entire cities in sin and silk. The might and blight of suggestion is not one to be taken lightly. Now, we caution, the honorable maiden must guard against the trend of the ailurophile. The effect begins in a most sly manner: most often, most ruinously, with the well-intended birthday gift of a pet cat. Within a week of frolicksome balls of string, the susceptible adolescent becomes an absolute disciple of the animal, following its convoluted wanderings through corridors and expressing a craving for cream, which the naïve parent willingly obliges. "I so adore my Tiger, my Max, my Kitty," gushes the youth. "What a perfect being! O! to be so lovely as that!" Soon enough the victim, engaging often in furtive purrs, will begin a sinuous procedure of curling around banisters and sleeping in a content orb in the

28

sunlight spilt upon the unraveling rug. The youth slinks
into an opaque night, padding noiselessly upon rooftops
and beneath the topiary, and returns with mouse blood
daubed upon the lips. Sphinxian and whorish eye-pencil
is used to accentuate the yellow stares and bottomless slits
of the pupils. When parents begin to notice such a crisis,
to yell and to plead and to wring their hands in desperate
sessions of family worship and fireside repentance, they are
met with superlative silence and the occasional scornful
mew. And no matter how firmly the adolescent shall be
disciplined, locked in an attic or sent to a gated school
which one ought to consider a true privilege, he or she
maintains that audacious ability to see in the dark, and so
escapes. Now, even as the gaslight emerges in coy dusk, we
see the youth grouped outside seedy taverns, in forbidden
gardens and alleyways like veins in times of passion: in
ecstatic desperation they wind about one another's lithe
bodies, yowling, shedding their gowns, lifting their tails.

See also **pandiculation**, **tibert**

agathodemon

(æɡəθəʊdiːmən) [adapted Greek ἀγαθδαίυων, from *agathdos*, ἀγαθδό-ς good + *daimon*, δαίυων a spirit] NOUN

A good divinity or genius, or one's good conscience.

(**1846** P. S BEAZLEY. *Fables of Exhaustion in Amoral Times*) **p 76** After fifty years, they had wearied of one another to a nearly intolerable degree, nigh unto the doldrums. Egbert came to find the agathodemon's voice to be an enormous irritant, and at times grew so exasperated with the unsolicited advice that he would break out in a rash peeling away in gleaming ichthyoidal flakes. The agathodemon, meanwhile, came to resent the lumpiness of Egbert's shoulder, which he had broken in a heavenly tumble from a cathedral's roof (a prank involving a gargoyle, very much against the agathodemon's counsel). So mostly they bickered; Egbert would eye a chocolate rabbit or a vaguely bewitched apple in the marketplace, and the agathodemon would warn him against the immorality of stealing, and if Egbert did purloin the desired object he would hear about it for days, and should he resist the urge he'd be bitter as lemon seed and full of grumbling soliloquies. And were Egbert to feign illness to escape his daily drudgeries, the agathodemon would flick his ear with a fingernail the size and feel of a thistle, and so Egbert would deliberately stand outside in the rain knowing well how his little companion despised the chill. Should Egbert devise a particularly mordant insult for a superior, he would receive a sermon upon politeness and how a word ought always be the caress of a silken glove. Egbert had lost a fair number of perspiring and forbidden loves by way of the agathodemon's sanctimonious murmurings, but then again, so had the agathodemon himself. How Egbert despised that self-righteous twittering, and how the agathodemon hated his host's summertime stink. Yet after so many decades of itchy and loyal annoyances, the pair simply could not bear to part. And so they remained, very virtuous and quite miserable.

See also **decumbiture, nemoral**

amphisbaena

(æmfɪsˈbiːnə) [Latin, adapted Greek *amphisbaina*, ἀμφίσβαιυα, from *amphis*, ἀμφίς both ways + *bainô*, βαίν-ειν to go] NOUN

A fabled serpent with a head at each end, capable of movement in either direction.

(**1533** ANONYMOUS. *Bestiarium Maestitia*) **p 3** For aye, the Serpente be a Serpente, but it be also a Book: a corrupt book indeed be the Amphisbaena. One Head speaketh solely in Rime, and tells of those Castles none save reptiles know, and of the Day the Hero storm'd the City whose streets as seen from below spelleth out our Deaths. So did the Romance end in a shower of grapes, sayeth the first. And still claimeth the other Head that the murder'r was always Gyltie, and yet shall be redeemed by the blessing of

a cat's chin; all be well, sayeth the one Head with a quille upon its tongue, and all be turmoil, sayeth the Other, and its hiss be script in water. And of the two Mouths of the Amphisbaena, we cannot know to which we must hearken, nor know which Adventure we must read and strain to live, until that day all things shalt come to their End.

See also **barghest, bucentaur, dipsas, disomus, homœoteleuton, mamuque, pyrausta, scytale, urisk, wasserman, yale**

amplexus

(æm'plɛksəs) [adapted Latin, *amplexus, amplecti,* embrace]
NOUN

The mating embrace of frogs or toads.

(**1799** BLOOR & TELEMACHUS. *Passion and Decomposition*) **p 58** And after those long days of propriety they struggled to sleep, fighting the insomnia of rational beings, while the dripping oaks and the vaguely glowing earth echoed with the low screams of the toads' amplexus, reminding them of that which they dared not be.

See also **catacoustics**

anachorism

(ənækərɪz(ə)m) [formed, to match *anachronism*, from Greek ἀνά back + χωρίου country, place] NOUN

Something geographically out-of-place, or foreign to a country.

(**1743** J. GINGELL & T. TOWNSHEND. *Accounts of the Thirteen Cities of Ememeer*, expanded ed.) **p 321** Let no antiquarian or shoemaker believe that t'was the map which betrayed the land. Such an incident would have been nothing new—duly recollect those days when the empire of the elephants was mistakenly drawn in a ring around the south pole, or the hundreds of primitive charts which absurdly misrepresented the lost continent as an ellipse hovering over eastern Mongolia. The people of the wondrous fourth city of Ememeer might have subdued a mere incorrect map; swiftly and suavely a committee would have accreted to print a glossy revision of the Unimpeachable Atlas, and dutifully would everybody cut a loyal index finger upon those pages dusted in gold. But 'twas the land that betrayed itself, and academia could do naught to salvage the final dignity of cartography. The first inconsistency arrived in the form of a hill like a dragon's terrible vertebra, which appeared at the edge of Ememeer one sweltering August dawn. None could recall having seen the hill before, and no preexisting survey bespoke its existence, but aye, there it swelled. The citizens of Ememeer might have allowed the anachorism to slip by, but within another holy week the river appeared, coursing down the city's main boulevard as veins run through our bone canyons. Soon hobgoblin

mountains were glimpsed sneaking on stone tiptoes along
the horizon, rumbling ever so slightly as they slid into a
novel scene. Forests obviously belonging to less rational
latitudes pranced upon an audacious southwestern breeze
and into pale plazas, and a rather insolent lake elected to
creep into everybody's favorite meadow, submerging the
lilies and the picnickers. The populace of Ememeer was
overwhelmed by inappropriate places, and though the
metropolis has sat forever as a compass rose blooming at
the heart of all its own maps, the people learnt now that
geography has its own set of instincts towards savage play.

See also **abature, caryatid, colubriferous, enantiodromia, fernticle,
filipendulous, halikeld, seismotherapy, turngree, xenia**

assoine

(əˈsɔɪn) [variant of *essoin*, verb, adapted Old French *essoigner*]
VERB

To make an excuse for someone's absence.

(1791 THIRD COUNCIL OF E., ET AL. *The Infinite Alibi*)
p 365 Please, do forgive our guest's unexpected delay; such
a punctual person she usually is. We understand that this
anticipation has likely seemed an endless taunt, that your
boredom has likely caused you horrible tummy gripes. We
do apologize for this, and assure you that she will soon
arrive. Naturally, such an anomalous nonappearance can
be nothing save justified. Our eminent guest's jeweled
pocket-watch has broken, and reads only the time at the
shimmering apex of the North Pole. She had to dash off
to the shop, fetching a pen and a sack of sugar beets. Upon
the needlessly complicated path through the murmurs of
the olive groves she was waylaid by a swarm of drunken
honeybees; she has lost her left shoe. She was forced to
make a quick debut at a plush pearlescent gala on the
moon. Afflicted with a brief bout of euphoric amnesia
after a meteoric impact upon her fontanelle, she for a time
believed herself to be the duchess of a genteel pack of
wolves, but the pestering southwest wind reminded her of
you. Again, we assoine, for we understand that as the wait
slides on and on into perpetuity, so too does the burden
of your accumulating memories wax into an ache like the
frown of a grandfather clock, but truly do we expect that
soon shall she arrive; she can explain.

See also **bocstaff, diatyposis, telarian**

balanoid

(ˈbælənɔɪd) [adapted Greek *balano-eides*, βαλαυοειδής, from *balanos*, βαλαυος acorn] NOUN

The shell of an acorn.

(**1801** DIVINE & FELTHAM, EDs. *Missives from the Faeries,* pt. III) **p 173** The question arises: is it form which follows function, or do we merely devise our elfin needs from the materials we are given, here in the quiet and generous loam? For one cannot deny that the balanoid represents the most sublime of hats.

See also **quercivorous**

barghest

('bɑːˌgɛst) [perhaps adapted German *berg-geist*, mountain-demon, gnome; or German *bahre*, bier, hearse, or German *bär*, bear] NOUN

A goblin which takes the form of a dog, appearing as an omen of death or misfortune.

(**1533** ANONYMOUS. *Bestiarium Maestitia*) **p 13** We shall dispute not the danger of the Barghest, and the glist'ning magick of its Fangs. For be it not true that the black hound bayeth 'mongst the grieving elms and walking stones upon the sinking skin of our kings' cemetery? And be it not known that London burn'd when the dogges arriv'd? O'er centuries we hath sought to guard ourselves from the harbinger of the descending Gloom, but we hath been but fools in error. For the finest defense 'gainst an evil sign be solely but to defeat it at its own fatefull Game. So shalt we seek to appear to the Barghest before it appears to us. We must creep upon the Beast as it sleeps in silken ashes, trace it through streets and o'er thatch, up a waterfall and 'neath the sighing bridge. For so surpris'd by its sight of us, we with our shimm'ring palms and crumbling shoes, the Barghest shalt do naught but accept us as mortall hints of its own Ruin.

See also **amphisbaena, bucentaur, dipsas, disomus, homœoteleuton, mamuque, pyrausta, scytale, urisk, wasserman, yale**

bibliotaph

('bɪblɪʊtæf) [adapted French *bibliotaphe*, from *biblio* + Greek τάφος tomb] NOUN

One who buries books by keeping them under lock and key, or other methods.

(**1824** M. ADRIAN. *Confessions Regarding Commendable Things*) **p 221** Of all books multifarious or obscure, 'tis this I love best of all. Past a floral frontispiece it commences with an epigraph in a tongue I have yet to decipher in full. Yet how I adore this old tome! Here is the tale of Emma the Bibliotaph, possibly fictional, elegantly set within a city of alabaster and palms, shrines to the patron saint of literate owls. Notorious is she, with her avarice, insolence, sheer ingenuity surpassing the cobra's deviance. The modern reader might blame her crime upon the manipulations of a malevolent star, or some obsessive affliction of swollen brain, or curiosity's lush sin. But in the city's vast library—its shelves, stacks, and guardian cats now long since incinerated unto a windstorm of whispering ash—she snatched the hieroglyphic nonsense of papyrus scrolls, binding them with sinew 'neath her gown. In the parlors of gracious friends she would call attention to a mouse dashing under the chaise lounge, and with that brief distraction pilfer her companions' volumes of trivia or scandalous tales. How grand, to read of Emma the Bibliotaph! Emma bartered clocks for erroneous atlases, and gambled away the fortunes of distant cousins for obsolete glossaries. Decent citizens at last began to

notice the absence of their treasures, but none could name
the scoundrel responsible, or where the loot might possibly
lie. Yet Emma's fatal flaw—as every proper heroine must
possess, vacillating at the whirlpool's brink—proved to be
her very affection for her plunder. Too arrogant and too
devoted she strode from her cellar to the deft barber to the
lavish marketplace, but realized not the rustling din of the
books hidden but glowing softly at her breast. Somebody—
probably a tabby—reported such audible evidence, and
with a great brandishing of sputtering torches the people
marched to apprehend and punish by undecided means
the criminal. Yet—O, what a magnificent yarn!—already
Emma was gone: none could say whitherto, whether she
had embedded herself among the ruby beetles and walking
sticks of a hollow oak tree, or chosen exile among in white
wastes, or if enraptured unto oblivion had simply vanished
into the index of a buried book. And moreover, never
was her stolen hoard unearthed; somewhere, I believe,
innumerable stories remain. Ambiguous and therefore
unending, this is my favorite tale. I should like to share
it—truly I would—but for the time I believe I shall keep
it, concealed against my exposed heart.

See also **latitant, vademecum**

bocstaff

('bɒkstɑːf) [Old English *bócstæf* corresponding to Old Saxon *bôcstaƀ*, Middle Dutch *boekstaf*, Old High German *buohstab*, Old Norse *bókstafr* , Swedish *bokstaf*, Danish *bogstav*; compare Gothic **bôkastafs*, from *bôk* writing-tablet + *staf-* staff, letter. According to some, originally 'beech-staff', but see also *book*] NOUN

A letter of an alphabet.

(**1791** THIRD COUNCIL OF E. ET AL. *The Infinite Excuse*) **p 249** The rumor is true, we shall now admit (for no brash and bullish circle of braggarts are we): a bocstaff has been lost. Admittedly, this represents a rather embarrassing dilemma, but as no solution has had the courtesy to present itself, we request now the assistance of thee, the people. We conjecture that the bocstaff was misplaced perhaps a month ago. We first noticed its disappearance in the agonizing, nocturnal composition of aimless romantic poetry (as so many other absences are oft detected), when the proper words needed to express a precise analogy for love in all its lambent and dark ineffability simply would not arrive. Our signatures grew slapdash and counterfeit, and in conversation we displayed a distinct inability to articulate deft synonyms for *red* or *staircase*, and witnessed the topsy-turvy confounding of the library's shivering spines. It may be the case that one of us merely dropped the bocstaff in one of our alphabetic ramblings, and should this prove the case, we shall accept our guilt in full humility. Mayhap one of us simply failed to close a satchel, and it slipped away along with a silk change purse (which we request be returned to us as well, if found). Mayhap one or all of us scribbled down a spontaneous idea in too much haste, so spoke in tones so singsong that the bocstaff scampered away in the manner of an absconding hare. Should we discover that the bocstaff harbored its own schemes to escape prior to the actual event, it shall be duly punished by drowning or a tomato-pummeled day in the stocks. Profusely we apologize, as its loss has made difficult the inscription of a goodly number of useful, sensuous words; we appreciate the public's patience with our error. But a substantial, appropriately epical reward shall be granted to any who might arrest the wretched, wayward thing, which even now is likely wandering between sordid taverns upon drunken serifs. It has occurred to us, also, that the bocstaff may have been stolen, and we imagine this bandit huddled in some despicable subterranean lair, gnawing upon a diacritical cookie and writing scandalous articles with cackling self-satisfaction. In light of such a possibility, we await the arrival of a repugnant ransom note, scrawled in a code of mockery and demanding things we do not yet understand.

See also **ætites, assoine, latitant**

bradypeptic

(brædɪˌpɛptɪk)   [from Greek *bradypepsia*, βραδυπεψία,
from *brady-*, βραδύ-ς, + *pepsis*, πεψ-ις, cooking or digestion]
ADJECTIVE

Slow of digestion.

(**1816**   E. E. NORDIN, ESQ.   *The True Adventures of
Emory, as told to E. E. Nordin*) **p 179**   As Emory came to
know all too well, the bradypeptic condition represents a
disease not wholly of stomach and belch, but moreover
of the windswept and electric chambers of memory. The
effects, true, are often belated—forty years in Emory's
case—but irrefutable.   For decades he did admittedly
experience sporadic bouts of apocalyptic stomachaches,
and gurgles which sounded quite frankly conversational,
but he disregarded the signs, blaming them upon poorly
made cheese or the recurrent bites of predatory butterflies.
But soon enough Emory's pains intensified, as such pains
and also exasperation are wont to do.   He turned first to
natural cures, a forced diet of bran and daily consumption
of the pages of a songbook, but these brought largely only
a sort of melodic boredom to his afternoons.   Having
heard marvelously sunny rumors, he gulped the fabled,
wizardly cure, the syrup of the diapente—berries and
elephant's sickled tusks, something suspiciously urinary and
something smelling of a desert caravan—and consequently
vomited.   The agonies grew only worse, and he lay stricken
by a roseate fever leaving him moaning and harassed by the
sound of unseen piccolos, capable only of vision in shades

of gold. He suffered finally a great digestive indignity at the base of a tree, producing a pile of vaguely volcanic waste; peering morbidly at the fetid artifacts of his belly and masking his nose against their miasma of secret foulness, he surmised that he had simply taken decades to digest this one thing: that ring which she had given to him those four decades past. He had forgotten whatever it was she had said. Stranger still, he could not at all recall swallowing the ring, but he supposed that something within him must have understood precisely what it meant.

See also **bucentaur**, **decumbiture**, **diapente**, **xanthopsia**

bucentaur

(bjuː ˈsɛntɔː(r)) [from the Italian, of uncertain origin, but from the Greek *buos*, βοῦς, ox + *kentauros*, κένταυρος, centaur, to form *bukentauros*, βουκένταυρος] NOUN

I. *The ship upon which on Ascension Day the Duke of Venice ritually sailed to wed the Adriatic Sea by dropping a ring into it,* or, 2. *A fabulous creature, half-human, half-ox, which is found nowhere in classical mythology but represented the figurehead of the ship itself.*

(1795 PYPER & VENNELLI. *A Historie of Romantick Miscellanie, incidents themselves being now mostly wrecked upon the rocks*) p 143 And when the duke murmured it: *yes*, the sea beneath grew as still as that verdant looking-glass through which we can see all of ourselves as we would exist in the contrary-world, and reflected in it were scattered the celestial asterisks and derelict constellations which upon most cool and pious nights we may never discern. We the mariners dropped our oars into the coral's waiting hands, and the salt fell as diamonds from our hardened skin. The sails drifted away on white wings. And when the duke dropped the ring over the starboard side, into the water like a mirror, like a mouth, we could not help but weep as it disappeared as a waning glint into the depths, to be swallowed by that great fish who survives solely upon

adoration given willingly, helplessly, forever.   Released
from our labors we watched then in glad anguish as the
bucentaur bowed its horned head and tautened its oaken
arms to pull us onwards, groaning under the weight of so
much love.*

See also **fremitus**, **quicquidlibet**, **ythe**

✣ NOTE Within the hidden Musæum Clausum,
in a room which is sometimes a colonnade of
clocks and sometimes an infinite lake, and
between the Transcendent Perfumes and the
Snake bred from human spinal marrow, there
is a pearlescent box without a definite bottom,
and in that box sits item number twenty: a
peculiar ring. The ring, reads a little placard
in an anonymous and irregular and vaguely
reptilian hand, was cut out of the belly of
a fish taken from the most abyssal portion
of the Adriatic, which smelled vaguely of
perspiration, widows' weeds, and perfume.

byss

(bɪˈs) [first senses onomatopoeic; also second from Latin *byssus*, fine flaxen cloth or asbestos, also third formed by removing the privative *a-* from *abyss*, forming *byssos*, βυσσος, depth or bottom of the sea] VERB, or, NOUN

1. *to sing or hum*, or, 2. *to hiss and crackle, as a fire*, or, 3. *fine linen*, or, 4. *the opposite of an abyss or void, that which has substance and attributes*, or, 5. *a word utilized by writers of Old English, to which is attached no certain definition.*

(**1711** R. F. GROVER. *An Old Woman in Norfolk, her distresses and how she solved them*) **p 191** That night, her song possessed no words to it, or rather none derived from our good and custom'ry English tongue, but nonetheless the old woman sensed that, aye, it did speak of something, and followed the crumbs of her own dry voice falling to the floor. She fingered the kerchief pulling her hoary hair back unto domestication, and rose to roll and rollick along the filaments of her song, kneeling before the fire that told its own sequence of sibilants, consonants, hard snaps. And of a sudden did it seem to her that the roof of her little hut peel'd back, as unfold the petals of flowers still unnamed, exposing their boundlessly frail pollen to the light and the dark. Looking up with waddled chin, helpless did the old woman fall backwards at the sight of the vault all a-dazzle. At once it became apparent that the true constellations were never merely connections of lonesome stars but in the holes between them, th'indefinable places in which no light can rescue the eye from its own love of sight; no title could she give to the shapes that careened towards a bony moon, none save for the Great Dog rabid in a western wilderness. O, she said to nobody at all, her mouth then moving silently in the search for what not-yet-invented words might explain what now she felt. For what had appeared sheer substance, the absolute byss of the sore sternum and flame and the pit of the plum, was naught save a reconfiguration of a nothingness which had come to mean something heartfelt to her, and what had seemed the terrible void, the absence of all stuff, was itself a real thing, the true existence of *not*. The old woman laughed, to nobody who was in fact somebody, merely not present at the time, and let fall the trailing threads of her kerchief as if abandoning a mourning veil; this felt lovely to her.

See also **hederated, i-what, vorago**

canicular

(kəˈnɪkjʊlə(r)) [adapted Latin *canīculār-is*, pertaining to the dog-star, from *canīcula*, little dog, dog-star, diminuative of *canis*, dog] ADJECTIVE

Pertaining to the days immediately preceding and following the heliacal rising of the Dog Star, Sirus, near or upon the 11th of August; of the "dog days" of summer.

(**1727** M. SARTORIUS. *Advanced theories of the new astronomy, and its perils*, first ed.) **p. 244** "We deny not the influence of the stars," writes Sir Thomas Browne. "We should affirm that all things were in all things, that heaven were but earth celestified, and earth but heaven terrestrified, that each part above has its influence on its divided affinity below." And so do we classify the canicular days—for always and ever must we seek to make of this world a consummate and animate encyclopædia—the dog days, those sweltering eras of summer when the wanton-toothed constellation of the Great Dog cavorts across the sky. Feral and devoid of intellect and clothes, we are pulled like prey to Sirius, that Dog Star, that lantern of the dire wolves, brightest of beasts roaming ravenous and foaming o'er the vulnerable earth. Among the hounds of slimy streets and gloaming, glowering woods we howl and gnaw upon swans' bones, and seeking one another's flesh wander mad across the wastes; we are star-struck and abject. Yet deny not the stellar mirror of the world; when with the cool palmistry of the first frost September beckons us home, so can we glimpse the Dog Star curling round its unseeable tail and pawing at a storybook, peering into the library with a whine like the guttering of a dying will o' the wisp, begging for a pun and a tale. For be it not said that Newton's ghostly gravity cannot help but apply to all bodies that shift and thrive and fast disintegrate in this universe?

See also lemyre, phasma

caryatid

(kærⲓætⲓd) [adapted Latin *caryātid-es*, pluralized Greek *Caraytis*, καρυάτις, a priestess of the goddess Artemis at the village of Caryae (καρύαι), hence a female figure] NOUN

A pillar shaped like a female form.

(**1743** J. GINGELL & T. TOWNSHEND. *Accounts of the Thirteen Cities of Ememeer,* expanded ed.) **p 89** In a din of hammers and bells the third city of Ememeer was raised that it might become an immortal home for its illustrious populace, a deliberate choreography of architecture speaking stonily of itself as the confluence of nobility and divinity, of mechanism and flesh, of the modern and the lingering myth of the past. To this end was money poured into the new omnipresent mirrors, the civic temples and unflagging lights and the inexhaustible fountains of rubies liquefied. And as was expected and desired and requisite, the finest of aristocrats arrived with trains of duly silent servants, and the money flittered forth and back

on little gilded wings. But as all agreed the finest aspect of Ememeer lay wholly in its stunning caryatids. For the city's ultimate theme was to be this sensuousness of stone, for clandestine and covetous, all did desire a resplendent maiden of marble to uphold the soaring rooftops of their endless lives. What was reckoned not, however, was that possibility that perhaps the people had been too virtuoso in their design. Thus 'twas all the more unexpected, all the more catastrophic, when at last the women of the columns heaved aside their burdens and departed in a clatter of rocky toes, and the city and the ruinous midnight fell upon everybody's heads.

See also **anachorism, colubriferous, enantiodromia, fernticle, filipendulous, seismotherapy, turngree, xenia**

catabibazon

(kætəbaɪbəzɒn) [Greek *katabibaxon*, *καταβιβαξόυ* bringing down, lowering] NOUN

In astronomy, the moon's descending node; also called Dragon's Tail.

(**Date indef.** M. CELESTE. *The Interpretation of Distance*)
p I Father, the moon does dance upon one round paw, and it is devoted to us. It is a fluid being, and it is fattened and forlorn with all the memory of salt. It is a monitor moon, and knows what it sees. Plucked from the sky, it is a cake composed wholly of confectioner's dust, and it is debris upon a musæum's hushed floor. The moon is voiceless, and it is keening, and it is booming and busting as the wealth of the tides rises and subsides. The gardener moon sows us, prunes us, uproots us from the ashen earth; the moon grows dizzy on milk. The wanderer moon becomes lost in the mist, and the ocular moon sees us all. It is a bent breastbone, gnawed by a starry dog. The moon's mind is sordid, and ignites the desire of oceans and cats, and its smiles illuminate our dreams in these mesmerized beds. Pupil of its own tearful eye, the moon is sympathetic

to our plight. This is the moon: sea of laughter telling stories to a child in the night, and also robber a-gallop over highway and hand. The moon is a tragicomedy in catabibazon, and the moon is unrequited love; the moon is omnipresent and it is not really there at all.

See also **aestites, bibliotaph, byss, catacoustics, interluculation, kermes, kirn, lemures, nubivagant, oudemian, rampick, rhyparography, seismotherapy, selenite, selenitic, tibert, ythe**

catacoustics

(kætə›kaʊstɪks) [from Latin *cata--* in sense of 'against and back from' + *acoustics*, study of sound. In French *catacoustique*] NOUN

The science of echoes, or other reflected sounds.

(**1945** H. WHITWORTH & T. TOOKER. *Catacoustics: A Plagiarized Primer.*) **p 76** The past hundred years constitute a century of fabulous advances in the field of catacoustics. Indeed, it has seemed as though not a single cake of a lunar month has gone by without some specialist unearthing a new and noteworthy breakthrough, some metamorphosis of the trembling pupae of our knowledge. Consider the momentous day when Professors Amira and Bab announced their detection of the wings upon which our resonances travel, or when Madame Gaspar published in the *Resonance Quarterly* the algorithm with which to calculate the maximum lifespan of an echo deprived of water. We now know the various effects of sound upon sundry fevers, and we have nearly completed our decoding of the ecstatic language of the dolphins. We have crafted laboratorial chambers in which we render our echoes quasi-sentient; C. T. Winslow reports that it is only a matter of time before we shall transform ourselves at will into bats. Of course, like any science, catacoustics is not without its pettiness: it seems at times as though the academies ring not with the clinks and simmerings of deft experiment but with the caterwauling spite of bickering experts, each claiming to be the first to happen upon a particular discovery. Such debates largely conclude with bitterness, rivalries, and poorly articulated insults. Yet there do exist those outliers who claim that in spite of all the strides of catacoustics, this apparent wealth of comprehension and revolution, it is in fact the case that all our innovations are only reiterations and reflections. In truth, they say, we revel in the mere reverberation of data, harmonic knowledge which has passed away and now returns to us.

See also **pheal**, **vespertilionize**

chiminage

('ʃɪmɪnədʒ) [adapted Old French *cheminage*, right of way, from *chemin*, road; in Law, Latin *chiminagium*] NOUN

A toll paid for passage through a forest.

(**1823** L. L. ELLERY. *Inconvenient Fees*) **p 136** Rates of chiminage have fluctuated over time and place, according to the demands of economics, the geology of social stratification, and the volatile politics of the faerie world. Lucretius records that the armies of Visigoths which swarmed Europe were taxed by the trees to the sum of some ten thousand elf-faced gold coins, which were buried in a glade in order to facilitate their dissolution. In the empire of the Aztecs, navigation through those jungles dripping with nectar and the copper scent of sacrifice was relayed by the jaguars, taking most often the form of an advance lament for the plumed pride of the Spaniards to come. The woods of northern India have traditionally demanded tribute of incense and red meat, to nourish the scrawny lions—now nearly extinct—who are the world's most assiduous foresters. In Siberia, the trees ask for cups full of transported seawater, and ask that the donation be accompanied by a formal gesture of gratitude, while in Scandinavia it is the wild geese who enforce the tax to the trees. In the sobbing and cambered forests of America, the past three hundred years have rendered the cedars too mournful to even utter their demands. In Ireland, the forests have disappeared, but once they offered passage in exchange for fiddling jigs. And the paths of the gallant stags cost nothing at all, but these are lost to our breakneck memory, neglecting the pleas of the ferns and the mosses' rainy embrace. Over centuries of fires and forgetfulness, however, the global debt which our species has incurred towards the woods has grown so vast, after so much was freely given and so much taken, and taken and taken unawares, that it becomes a wonder that we can stand at even the gloomy brink of any bastion of trees without hearing from the creaking boughs their desperate wails for recompense.

See also **abature, dendrolatous, diatyposis, interlucation, nemoral, nervure, porraceous, rampick**

chirm

(tʃɜːm) [Old English *cirm-an,* to cry out, shout, make a noise. Compare Dutch *kermen,* Middle Dutch *kermen, karmen,* to mourn, lament, Middle Low German *kermen.* The ulterior history is uncertain]

NOUN I. *A collective term for goldfinches,* or, 2. *The mingled din of many voices,* or, VERB 3. *To cry out in a chatter or warbling like that of birds.*

(**1747** Z. PROTHERA & E.M.BAYLEAF. *Chronicles of the Avian Wars,* volume V) **p 676** Not since the height of the Avian Wars has this word enjoyed much wide usage, but indeed was there a time when people had much to fear from the chirms. While amidst the birds' twittering armies it was the herons who proved the most useful strategists, and the condors with their brazen enormity who fought at the front lines, and paradoxically the turtledoves who from on high commanded the feathered engines of war, the chirms were truly something terrifying to behold. Some scholars have recorded the chirms' most ingenious mode of approach, that susurrus of terror congealing slowly in a soldier's ear until one understood that death approached on wings like blades of butter. Of all the ornithological beings, the goldfinches alone were capable of gripping in their delicate claws a fearsome sword, swinging it left and right as dictated by the savagery of wind. And in spite of the birds' defeat at human hands—and the subsequent razing of their incomparable nests to make room for the castles which would eventually dissolve into suburban murk—the chirms remain a chilling historical ghoul. And memory sings in wordplay. 'Tis for this reason that we at times experience an ancestral shudder, when, in everyday commemoration of those subtle murderers, a bird chirps.

See also **engastration, kae, shiterow, tectrix**

chorizont

(kɔərɪ›zɒnt) [adapted Greek *chorizontes*, χωρίζουτ, from *chorizen*, χωρίζεν, to separate] NOUN

One who disputes the authenticity of an author's identity (originally, ascribing the Iliad *and the* Odyssey *to two different authors).*

(**1859** O. GARDNER. *Revision and Blame*) **p II** You know not the numbered page upon which you pause now in breathlessness, nor how many chapters of trauma or deliverance remain. But surely you will be written as protagonist through each sudden twist of ankle and plot. Backwards through what you call the rustling past, you recollect the alluring introduction, strewn with carnations and candle wax, and the description of your own inimitable (you are certain) character—easily startled, brave in the presence of thunder, drawn to details irrelevant—before you become it. Somewhere, you know you might find your parents: the one who read to you upon a wild patchwork quilt, and the one who collected teacups of blue willow and seemed to conceal a secret, perpetual unhappiness. *She loved them,* it is written. You might be envisaged from outside yourself. *She was born by night, she hated him, she held in cupped hands the dying wren.* At times your motivations and metatarsals occur in present tense, yet at others you think of your biography as the warped evolution of past perfect retrospect; all memory is anachronism. And so you have begun to doubt that the Author is who the author is said to be. For no reliable narrator would permit your mood swings and palpitating contradictions: how can you quiver with simultaneous adoration and revulsion for a villainous romantic interest? Who lets you recollect your long-ago bedchamber as walled in blue, when it has been written as the crimson of a nonexistent rose? No writer of any laudable talent or name—perhaps a child, an idiot, a wild goose with ink upon feral quill, or else a spectrum of authors wavering and cruel, together toying with history in a pitiless poetic game. The motif of blue willow and foreshadowed arsenic poisoning appear too often for mathematic law, and you seem to function as a metaphor for some fundamental, failing human quest. With antiquated gravity somebody has claimed that there will come a page whereupon all words cease, leaving an arctic wilderness of blank paper with the aurora tinkling blind above. What will become of you? Some passages suggest that you are a character forever contradicting yourself, in which case it would seem not improbable that you are the chorizont forever writing your own world, in which case, you must decide now the meaning of the moth lying dead and lunar at the windowpane.

See also **bocstaff, homœoteleuton, rifacimento**

cidentine

('sɪdɛntɪn) [A word invented in 1653 by Scottish writer Sir Thomas Urquhart for the express purpose of his translations of the works of the French author François Rabelais] ADJECTIVE

South of the teeth.

(**1800** D. MOTTERSHEAD. *The possible geography, in which many surprising things shall come to light, with a new introduction*)

p 157 A laurel for Sir Thomas Urquhart—a man who from mathematical figments constructed his own trigonometry comprehensible to nobody else, who as a joke created a vitriolic and absurd universal language in which one could refer to eleven genders and five moods with which to discuss herbs. Notable may be the fact that this man died of laughter. Praise be to Urquhart, the gypsy of verbosity, sending missives to we in our immobilized chairs—lacking cartography and lacking proof, so nonetheless does he write, "just as we have the Countreys with us cisalpine, being south of the Alps, and transalpine, so far across their peaks, so have they there the Countreys cidentine and transdentine, that is, behither and beyond the teeth." And from our quite-serious seats we may infer from such an account that in our mouths there exists a vast and complex world, a volatile territory of tongue divided into the proud nations of various flavors, sores, and syllables; oh, we are not so dull as we have thought. Indeed, there roam within a hundred thousand invisible citizens, whispering wet battle cries and fighting one another for command of this realm of eating and laughter, speech and the slow kiss, a place wherein all things are transformed.

See also **anachorism**, **frantling**

colubriferous

('kɒljʊbrɪfərəs) [from Latin *colubrifer*, from *colubr(i)*-, snake + *-fer*, bearing + *-ous*, from Latin *ōsus*, suffix denoting 'full of, abounding in'] ADJECTIVE

Bearing or bringing forth snakes.

(**1743** J. GINGELL & T. TOWNSHEND. *Accounts of the Thirteen Cities of Ememeer,* expanded ed.) **p 219**   Ne'er was it ascertained as to whom among the citizens of the seventh city of Ememeer might be held responsible for the colubriferous calamity, though as admitted by the feeble zoologists the question could hardly have made a difference. 'Twas conjectured that someone must have left a needle in a platter of milk to curdle upon a veranda.   Or perhaps, some said, the city had been built in the exact path of the magnetic boulevards along which rings the cosmognosis, that enigmatic call summoning all creatures towards auroral migration.   It may have been more probable that some imbecile or misanthrope had spoken a summoning word, which no one could determine or pronounce but which was surely quite sibilant.   Perhaps a cat had walked backwards on a piano.   But no matter—for it grew soon clear that Ememeer faced an insurmountable disaster, as the serpents began to advance upon the city, slithering through the gutters, curling up to aestivate in desk drawers, laying speckles

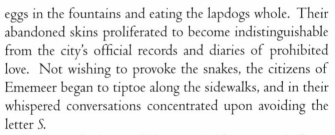
eggs in the fountains and eating the lapdogs whole. Their abandoned skins proliferated to become indistinguishable from the city's official records and diaries of prohibited love. Not wishing to provoke the snakes, the citizens of Ememeer began to tiptoe along the sidewalks, and in their whispered conversations concentrated upon avoiding the letter *S*.

See also **anachorism, amphisbaena, caryatid, cosmognosis, dipsas, enantiodromia, fernticle, filipendulous, scytale, seismotherapy, turngree, xenia**

coquelicot

('kəʊklɪˌkəʊ) [adopted French; the name of the red poppy, and hence of its color] NOUN, or, ADJECTIVE

A brilliant color being an admixture of red and orange, the hue of the common Red Poppy.

(1751 H. MALLORIE. *Queen Flora*, act II, scene V**) p 33**

QUEEN: Find the now a poppy red
Equal to coquelicot!
LAVINIA: I seek with blinded eyes.
QUEEN: Find for me the living bloom—else find
Fore'er was the word a lie, and this we ne'er knew.
Slaves thus, abandon we our empty names
To the predominance of stars!

See also **kermes, porphyrogenite, porraceous, watchet, xanthopsia**

corbicula

(kɔːˈbɪkjuːlə)   [Latin *corbicula*, diminuative of *corbis* basket]
NOUN

A part of the hinder leg of a bee specially adapted to carrying pollen.

(**1944** C. N. O'DUINN. *Le Petit Biologique*) **p 171** Of
what divisions are we capable? As we ask ourselves what
vast cosmologies we might construct for our stargazing
selves, so too must we ask what heavenly miniaturization
we might achieve. For inextricable from the existence of
intricate things is our ability to partition them, and to
name the fragments left behind. And in turn do we divide
these pieces unto more and more shards of their own; the
planet sliced unto the animate electricity of life and life
sliced unto animality, and animality unto entomological,
entomological unto order *Hymenoptera* and thusly unto

body of bee and bee unto leg, leg unto corbicula and unto these slivers of the exoskeleton, onward smaller and smaller unto a gleaming black joint, dusted with gold and fertility. But how to what infinitesimal extent may we divide this? On and on and on unto cells, unto acids, unto spirals and molecules and the frenzies of atoms and the trembling particles which defy the principles of space—and onwards perhaps unto an miniscule fragment existing just beneath the level of a twittering neutrino, past a thought? Is there no limit to smallness, or at some point within all things will we run into an unknowable wall?

See also **garguill**, **ycore**

corbin

(ˈkɔːˌbɪn) [from Old English *corb* or *corbel*, raven, Old French *corbin*; also see Latin *corv-us*, raven] NOUN

1. *A raven*, or, 2. *the "raven-bone," the lowest point of the breastbone of a deer.*

(**1703** M. SHIPSEY. *How came the fawns in spring*) **p 201** So goes the covenant: the raven shall lend its name to the deer's swift and pearly skeleton, screening the heart with a word crafted of feathers black. And in hushed exchange, the other consents to die. Thus it is that in the gently dire groves where the stones hum their own long biographies, there lies the corpse of the deer in decay, crowned by horns ephemeral as bone lightning. Nestled within the bloodied ribcage is the raven, pecking at this final bit of body and hungering for the memory of its own name.

See also **abature, garguill, inquiline, ziczac**

cosmognosis

(kɒzməʊgˌnəʊsɪs) [from Greek *cosmo-*, κόσμος, universe + gnosis, γνῶσις, knowledge] NOUN

That instinct which incites an animal to migrate at a particular time of year to a particular place.

(**1816** D. V. ROSETTI. *Lament of a Vagrant Naturalist*)
p 447 I cannot divine why it is that I can hear it not. Have I not my ears like nautili, the smallest of golden bones twinkling within? Is this not unjust? With insomniac spasms am I am certain that the cosmognosis must be a melody akin to the voice of familiar foreigners within our dreams, or to a climax, or a knowledge of all things. The geese discern it, I understand, for as October moodily descends they gather in their trigonometric grace to seek out the antipodes; should I survive to the murmuring crocuses of spring I am certain I shall witness their return, upon the next ring of the cosmognosis. And in August the cicadas went mad, making translucent, violent love in the weeds and burying themselves in the blackened earth; and each year the deer intuit which ivy to eat and which chalky path they must follow into the sheltering hills. I hypothesize the existence of some seasonal song informing the beasts of that-which-must-be-done. Otherwise how might the bears waddle their fattened way into cavernous beds? Mayhap this planet's magnetic cobweb, the triplicate romance between north and south and iron, emits its own natural cry—the compass rose as flower given voice. Yet if this great noise be so global, then why may I catch none

of its strains? I should like to hear this sound before I fall unto my final dust, but as of now I exist only in silence, that electric quiet which precedes an August storm, the wordlessness of slumbering pheasants and rotting leaves.

See also **abature, holophanerous**

decumbiture

(dɪˌkʌmbɪtjʊə(r))   [An irregular formation from Latin *dēcumbĕre*, to lie down; the etymological form being *decubiture*]
NOUN

1. *the act of taking to bed in illness*, or, 2. *an astronomically prescribed statue constructed above a sickbed in order to prognosticate recovery or death.*

(**1816** E. E. NORDIN, ESQ. *The True Adventures of Emory, as told to E. E. Nordin*) **p 216** Emory suspected his malady to be the questionably amorous result of an infected engagement ring, or perhaps of the acute bite of a carnivorous butterfly. There was no telling how long it might have incubated within him, this golden bacterium or venomous nectar, bubonic gnome or whatever it was, but he was incapacitated from aching head to moldering toes. Prodigious bile had him heaving over a washbasin, and he displayed also highly artistic blotches and toenails like deceased fish. He suffered chills and ghoulish aches, and his fever was of a solar degree. Gulping an alchemical tea of bayberries and powdered ivory, the rank urine of a wildcat, myrrh still heady with the treacherous aromas of faraway sandstorms, which previously he had sampled and thoroughly disliked, Emory took to his bed with a hot water bottle clutched to heaving gut. Not until after his seventeenth consecutive nap did Emory notice the figure perched dim and indifferent upon the bedpost, its character unfathomable: shape devoid of substance, form without matter, shade without stuff. Though at first he yelped and took meager refuge in

73

a heap of pillows, he found himself humbly resigned—a biography of complaint, he reasoned sullenly, and gloom for a nursemaid. But the figure seemed not particularly unfriendly, only rather serious, and something of a boon in the midst of bedridden boredom. 'Twas rather pleasant to gain a little company, and so Emory and the decumbiture lounged side by unintelligible side, nibbling upon toast and gambling with merrily sinister tarot cards.

See also **bradypeptic, diapente, xanthopsia**

dendrolatry

(dɛn›drɒlətrɪ) [from Greek *dendron*, δένδρον, tree, + *-latry*, Greek λατρεία , worship] NOUN

The worship of trees.

(**1502** TRANSLATED P. EBELTHITE, FROM KOLOIOS III. *Apologia Kalliphthogos*) **p 467** O Cypresse, thou Dyrge of Cliffe, of Grove, bee thou the highth of all mine funerall crys, thou of ruefull leaf and greene solemnitie. The Fyre hath taken my Love. Standst thou afore me, Cypress, for I be one of this Leygue of Mourners, wee of bless'd Dendrolatry who beat our breasts mongst th'impending thunder-storms. Kneyl I now at this the verge of our Cemeterie to come, for I canst comprehend not mine griefe, nay, without the Voyce of thy whisp'ring boughs.

See also **chiminage, diatyposis, interlucation, nemoral, nervure, porraceous, rampick**

diapente

(daɪə›pɛnti:) [adopted from Old French, from Latin *diapente*, Greek *διά πέντε χορδῶν συμφωνία*, 'the harmony between five strings'] NOUN

1. *A medicine composed of five ingredients*, or, 2. *As used in ancient and medieval music, the harmony or consonance of a perfect fifth interval.*

(**1581** M. N. SPRAT. *Emptiness of the Teaspoon*) **p 44** To the cauldron the Wizarde addeth Fair Ivorie, streak'd with still the tears of those Oliphaunts, who of all creatures be the last remaining bodies to witness true the Tragedie of the Stars. He addeth Bayberrys, that tasteth of such Blue deliciousness he can do naught save devour, and lick the Juices from his hands 'til the Tongues be bruis'd. The Apprentice stirreth the steaming Brew counter-clockwise, as Witchery doth dictate, and the Wizarde distilleth in't a trickle of the enchanted Pysse of the Wilde Lynx; then cometh Myrrh, the balm which maketh all skin as soft as the Dragonflys' Kiss. But what be the fifth Ingredient? The diapente boileth, but incomplete it be, and unto its completion the Wizarde knoweth he shall find no Cure. For he doth know that for the Full Effecte he must contribute the Name, a Burning Letter which shall signal the height of all stars and little things. With a flame of Quicksilver and weeping as do the moon's doves, he lighteth aflame and shall consign to ash and give to the Diapente the word he hath written 'pon a scrap of birch-bark: 'tis the Name of somebodie he hath Loved.

See also **bradypeptic, decumbiture, lygure, quintan**

diatyposis

('daɪətaɪpəʊsɪs) [adopted Latin, adapted Greek rhetorical term *diatuposis,* διατύπωσις, a vivid description, from *diatupo-ein,* διατυπό-ειν, to form or represent perfectly] NOUN

A perfect description.

(**1722** V. KELEHER. *Ode and Adversary*) **p 82** The heroine shall arrive in a shower of lilacs so as to smother the ladybirds sleep-creeping with upon the bloodied earth; she will call their freckled scarlet shells back unto life. We shall know her by the mark like the lush stellar nova of a fern scarring upon her unbreakable jaw, and her coronet of vines o'er black waterfall hair. Thus is it written, and thus shall she come. Without spear or sword inscribed by the elfin charms of wizards in despair, without crossbow or grandiose cannonball shall she bear arrows crafted of papyrus rewritten, and shrink not when over her the dark waters arise. All these horrors—the putrefaction of small kindnesses, the venom tainting the diluted clouds of changing skies, the incessant hunger and voracity and torture in the long grass—these she shall face, and with floral hands bless our brows and forgive us that we cannot ourselves confront them. But the best of us lack all conviction, one of us shall say, the worst full of passionate intensity. Her arms shall be ophidian, clavicles meteoric and bearing a fissure in her breast, and her feet shall shimmer as do the fish, her face resembling strangely our own sisters who were stillborn. Children will wish to wed her, and the old wish to slumber at her side, and o'er us her dreams of infant falcons will hoot in tune with waxing moon. We can stop fighting now. She will smell dizzy as alchemy, and kissing her fingers we shall taste beeswax in May. Her voice recollects those of dead bards, and proclaims that never did we need our knives; she is all we have been certain we might be and everything we dare not become. We shall sense she fears more than she admits. And yet we are afraid, for if, now, we venture to complete her diatyposis, thus shall she become real.

See also **assoine**

dipsas

(ˈdɪpsæs) [Latin *dipsas*, Greek δίψας, originally adjective 'causing thirst'] NOUN

A fabled serpent whose bite produces a raging thirst.

(**1533**   Anonymous. *Bestiarium Maestitia*) **p 3** We are tolden that the Dipsas be like a Flatterer, but only once have we looked upon't, 'neath the Rock of Journeys in that red desert where the Thunder shall ne'er cease. From its cavern there did come a little Hissying. We couldst see naught but glimm'ring eyes, but nor could we depart, for be we not tolden that the want for Praise resembleth so the ache of Thirst?

See also **amphisbaena, barghest, bucentaur, disomus, jornada, mamuque, pyrausta, scytale, urisk, wasserman, yale**

disomus

(daɪˌsəʊməs) [from *disomatous*, two-bodied, from Greek δισώματ-ος, double-bodied (from δι-, two + *somat*, σώματ, body) + *-ous*, from Latin *ōsus*, suffix denoting 'full of, abounding in'] NOUN

A monster with two bodies.

(**1533** ANONYMOUS. *Bestiarium Maestitia*) **p 6** We be not afeard of the Disomus, though we be tolden we ought. It be said that 'tis the Monstrous Deviants of our Custom'ry Bodies and Wonderfull Self which of all things shall ghast us most, and we think glimpse such fiends acrouch behind barns, 'pon those nights whence the Moon be fattened. But behold thee the Disomus! and shinketh not. There be no head to holden dreadfull Teeth, no eyes of Rancor most terrifying. Two furr'd Bottoms do tug upon one another in fool desperation, and two peculiar Tails but twitch in Furie. And so the bound Rumps struggle on without end, which we read to be sure the Metafore for the eternal Wretched Things of this world.

See also **amphisbaena, barghest, bucentaur, dipsas, mamuque, pyrausta, scytale, urisk, wasserman, yale**

ecuelle

(eɪkɔwɛl) [adopted French *écuelle*: while uncertain, popular Latin source is inferred to exist as *scūtella*] NOUN

A two-handled bowl for soup or porridge.

(**1830** B. J. FETTIPLACE. *Life Among the Oats Continued: Elmer's Maturity*) **p 322** Quite frankly, Elmer had labored unflaggingly at the porridge plant for far too long a time, and so he knew that at last he surely merited the award. It had been four tumultuous decades of wormy agrarian crises and freak winters, forty years spent laboring over the vats of this cavernous factory with its smokestacks brimming with goop. It was his frantic pedaling which turned the groaning wheels which milled the oats, and his sweat which mingled as priceless salt with the grains. Elmer had been the one to revolutionize the culinary process by crafting the equation with which to gauge the most flawless proportions of oatmeal, water, and goats' milk, and therefore it was he who was responsible for the warmed cheeks of multitudes of delighted children and toothless old women gumming their food and murmuring incoherent nursery rhymes. And who selected, out of three hundred delectable species, the sweetest and most shriveled breed of raisin for the breakfast table? None but Elmer, indeed. He had toiled there for forty years, and therefore he did not believe himself to be unjustified in demanding now, upon retirement, his honorary ecuelle, that golden trophy which is not merely a bowl, no, sir, not merely a bowl into which one pours one's clumpy porridge, but a bowl into which he would pour his grueling years.

See also **wangrace**

edaphon

('ɛdəfɒn) [German (coined in biologist R. Francé's *Das Edaphon* (1913)), from Greek ἔδαφ-ος, floor + *-on*, pluralizing suffix] NOUN

The community of organisms dwelling in soil.

(**1915**   G. JENET. *Autochthonic Biology: Confessions in the Dark*) **p 776**   Dwelling here, beneath the foundations of your home with all its architectural sanity and its symbolic cornerstone, we have possessed ample time to learn all about you. Buried deep in the black earth as are the first feverish memories of lust, we detect through vibrations subsonic and *basso profundo* the tremors of what you call the world: we have known the meticulous grain-by-glittering-grain formation of sandstone, and seismic revolutions overturning isles in the lonesome and unnamed, the subtle groaning of the planet's spin—and the resonance of everything you do. You walk with heavy heels when slipping from the ambrosial dreams dripping out of your bed, and often arrive at the bottom of the sweeping stair only to forget that which you desired in the first place. We perceive the weight of your shining new purchases, the bending of floorboards when you acquire a cabinet whose whorled woodwork proved too lovely for you to resist— loudly you excuse yourself. By noisy accident you slam the doors, the bang descending to rattle our keen teeth, and your wailing, ecstatic arguments with your wayward love. But when you are alone we catch the echoes of your exuberantly discordant voice as you sing along to your favorite maudlin jazz tunes, and you dance with leaps lacking all rhyme. We the archaeologists subterranean, we the edaphon, are fascinated by you and your aery, passionate life, and listening while just above the rich dirt you chatter to yourself at paranoiac midnight, we desire very much to unearth you and glimpse at last your exquisite toes.

See also **catacoustics**

enantiodromia

(ɛnˌæntɪəʊˈdrəʊmɪə)   [adapted Greek ἐναντιοδρομία, running in contrary ways] NOUN

The process wherein a thing is replaced by its opposite, and the subsequent interaction of the two.

(**1743** J. GINGELL & T. TOWNSHEND. *Accounts of the Thirteen Cities of Ememeer,* expanded ed.) **p 801** The enantiodroma of the ninth city of Ememeer began with the chocolate—for o'er one opaque night, with the suddenness most often attributed to the whim of harps in thunderstorm, the bulbous cordials decaying softly in a banquet's debris transformed suddenly into cubes of salt, which spoiled several leftover romances. 'Twas odd indeed, but simple enough to ignore under the pretense of some novel culinary style, until one day all the exotic carpets with their plush flatness became lofty, palatial houses, their doors unopened and unlocked. That same afternoon each authenticated encyclopedia turned to entirely false biographies of affluent celebrities. The baker's cardiac breads became arrays of slumbering badgers, and shoes were no longer shoes but paper birds built to fly towards droning Saturn. The following day, Ememeer's immensely popular games of checkers—red and black in their eternal geometrical war—were entirely transmogrified into tools of empire, so that thrice-kinged victors jumped into their own ruin and politics were destabilized by play. Lilacs were at once cannonballs. And the cats licked themselves until they took on the forms of dogs made of water, and the ornamental figs cast shadows which were pure and tangible flame, their upturned roots emerging from a new firmament of glittering dirt overhanging the city: an Orion's belt of earthworms, comets which were compost, Polaris as a function of a poppy.

See also **anachorism, caryatid, colubriferous, fernticle, filipendulous, seismotherapy, turngree, xenia**

encardion

(ɛnkɑːdɪən) [adapted Greek *ἐγκάρδιον*, the heart or core of wood] NOUN

The pith of a vegetable.

(**1828** O. SCILLITOE. *The Vegetables of Great Reality*) **p 500**
Duly note, then: 1. the encardions of the unripe cabbages, in which are curled certain beings (lying in wait, as a shadow conceals its intent at panoptic noon), who to pass the time before the lush unfolding to write anagrams in dew, or, 2. the encardions of the pea pods, long known to be the havens of little green lovers, or, 3. the encardions of onions, which may quite possibly (as we lack any proof to the contrary) spiral within themselves deep unto the acrid heart of an as-yet-unbloomed universe, inducing the inevitable tears.

See also **latitant, tribuloid**

engastration

(ɛngæˈstreɪʃən) [from Greek ἐν, in + *gasteo*, γαστερ, belly + from Latin *–ātiōn*, denoting action] NOUN

The stuffing of a bird inside another.

(**1747** Z. PROTHERA & E.M.BAYLEAF. *Chronicles of the Avian Wars*, volume III) **p 464** One can imagine indeed the terror of the ornithologists upon the engastration's squelching boom, at once the bloated pheasants opened their beaks, and thence emerged the finches, the thrushes, the baby jackdaws, one grimy magpie, and a sprinkling of rather sticky hummingbirds.

See also **chirm, kae, shiterow**

eutrapely

(ɣtræpɛli:) [adapted Greek εὐτραπελία, from εὐτραπελος, pleasant in conversation, from εὖ, well + τρέπειν to turn. The Greek word is used by Aristotle for 'pleasantness in conversation,' one of his seven moral virtues; also representing a reprehensible levity of speech or 'jesting'] NOUN

Eloquent or witty conversation.

(**1711** T. PERKINS. *Many Enjoyable Conversations, and Comments Which May Be Employed: A Guide*) **p 53** A reminder: as "eutrapely" is itself a rather eloquent and witty word, should one venture so far as to drop it casually in an actual eloquent or witty conversation, one shall in fact quite drolly negate all existence.

See also **i-hwat**

fernticle

('fɜ:ntɪk(ə)l)   [dialect, from *fern*, previous spelling *farntikylle*]
NOUN

A freckle whose shape resembles a fern.

(1743   J. GINGELL & T. TOWNSHEND.   *Accounts
of the Thirteen Cities of Ememeer*, expanded ed.) **p 1072**   As
was foretold in the tenth city of Ememeer, the one for
whom the people so earnestly waited was to be known
by the fernticle. This was confirmed not only by their
most prodigious form of prediction, this being divination
through the migratory triangles of screaming birds,
corroborated by the undeniable artistry of mathematics.
Like a burning letter the fernticle would signal the coming
culmination of all hopes. As such, the people all watched
for it, for they were all of them citizens of the future
and the age of automatons and fulfillment. And aye,
in time somebody came forth to point out the mark on
her transparent forearm. Following examination, it was
agreed that the tendrilled form of the pigmentation might
well amount to a fernticle, but the thing could also be
considered the image of a winter star. And hence another
made his own naked debut, bearing a splotch on the sole of
his grubby foot, and this too seemed probable enough. But
then somebody displayed a sporelike spot secreted on his
inner thigh, though the question was raised as to whether
this was not a fernticle at all but the scar of certain (quite
enjoyable) adventures. And then there was that blemish
upon the nape of a magnificent neck, and the havoc

began, as the people realized the tremendous and electric potential of skin. They sought it upon themselves and one another, sneaking into lavatories to inspect themselves or the downy backsides of chance companions. Soon enough, all were enraptured by the absolute epidemic of fernticles, enthralled in the endless process of running eyes and hands over the scars and perfect flaws of one another's bodies, until forgetting wholly that thing which they had sought.

See also **anachorism, assoine, caryatid, enantiodromia, filipendulous, nucha, seismotherapy, turngree, xenia**

filipendulous

(fɪlɪˈpɛndjʊləs) [from Latin *filipendul-us*, from *filum*, thread + *pendulus*, hanging] ADJECTIVE

Hanging by a thread.

(**1743** J. GINGELL & T. TOWNSHEND. *Accounts of the Thirteen Cities of Ememeer,* expanded ed.) **p 901** 'Twas one terrible August, whilst the heat's depravity caused fragments of certain constellations to break from the filigreed sky to plop into pitchers of lemonade, when the spiders conquered the eighth city of Ememeer. Ememeer,

harried for so long by dairy allergies and unwarranted cyclones, had of late lolled in a welcome stretch of quiet wealth; a supremely thick wall had been erected around the city, warding away even the slightest sulfurous chance of dragons and burning ideas. But no one had expected the spiders, who seemed to generate themselves with the spontaneity of a wicked laugh within the city itself. The arachnids emerged in spurts from the unexplored cellars, and poured out of the chimneys in an entourage of ash, and when the daisies bloomed they unfolded with infant widows whimpering in the pollen. They proceeded then to craft their webs with arcane complexity, from pillar to angelic pillar on the new city hall, in lush bedchambers, over the whitewashed chapels and betwixt the susurrating pages of unread books. Extermination, when attempted, proved noxious to Ememeer itself, for to rid oneself of that which emerges from one's own heart is not a possible task. Veils of cobwebs muted the sun, admitting naught save the dwindling of red stars, and things only worsened as the spiders burped up a daily glut of eggs. Beneath the accumulated weight of gossamer the filipendulous city began to crumble, and so the lesson of the spiders was revealed, for indeed did it become obvious that all had been forever suspended over the chasm of their own destruction.

See also **anachorism, caryatid, colubriferous, enantiodromia, fernticle, seismotherapy, telarian, turngree, xenia**

frantling

(fræntlɪŋ) [a nonsense word invented in 1693 by Scottish writer Sir Thomas Urquhart for the express purpose of his continued translations of the works of the French author François Rabelais] NOUN

The mating cry of a peacock.

(**1891** ROSEBLADE & GILFEATHER. *A Diary of Love among the Early Dead, and Childhood Lost*) **p 276** It was this that infuriated me most of all, and I could understand not how you might possibly find the noise no irritant, not sand within the ear's soft nautilus, but rather some sort of fitful

and charmed melody to which you sang along. In demi-
blindness I recall how each morning the peacocks preceded
the dawn, as if too splendid to walk behind a thing so
mediocre as the sun, that rotund marquis shambling
towards its daily duties. And how I awoke with brows
already inscribed by a frown, and required a whole hour
to rub the diamonds and mucus of slumber from my face.
How the peacocks copulated with noise and convulsions,
visible to us only as luminous flourishes stalking in spasms
just beyond the grass, their unfurled plumes a transgression,
an emerald assault, a dream we were told was a crime. But
how you pursued them, pattering a rhythm of laughter
over moss and sandbank, with diminutive daisies sprouting
where your feet had met the earth. How you could never
catch the peacocks; how I threw stones and never struck
their breasts; how you would balance the point of a single
exuberant feather upon your palm. How I slowly gained
the disquieting and iridescent sense that those passionate
frantlings were always meant for you, that the lyricism of
mating could cross species and sky for your sake alone,
and that the black raindrop of a peacock's gaze—and its
further host of false and lustrous and exemplary eyes—
could see what was to come.

See also **homœoteleuton**, **nucha**, **supernatant**

frazil

(freɪˈzɪl) [a Canadian adaptation of French *fraisil*, coal-dust, cinders] NOUN

A layer of ice at the bottom of a stream.

(**1910** T. T. CATTO. *Excursion to the Pole*) **p 230** Passion is not by necessity an elevated temperature, and some sorts of metaphoric fevers are deliriums of hypothermia— or we may rearrange ourselves to see it so. Say that the cold possesses its own eroticism. Say that there exists an intrinsic sensuality belonging to the icy horsetails of comets, adventurers in the vacuum. Wooly mammoths are libertine, and the Arctic is a bawdy-house of burlesque aurora and lecherous polar bears. Frostbite is the surrender of the extremities to temptation. The winter solstice is bacchanalia with the scant lace of frost. Glaciers groan with sliding scandals, and snowflakes are frankly pornographic. Say that this is why one discovers lovers caught and crystallized within the frazil, blue lips parted as if in an ultimate gasp, breasts wrapped in the last eels of November; there they rest, petrified in the stratum of poignant ice that underlies the water, as one body hums beneath the other.

See also **gelatia**

fremitus

(ˈfrɛmɪtəs) [Latin, from *fremerĕ*, to roar] NOUN

1. *A dull roaring noise*, or, 2. *a palpable vibration or thrill on the walls of the chest.*

(**1813** RAINSBURY & SABINE. *Daily Exercises for the Beginning Lyricist, or the mathematician inclined to pay attention to words*) **p 242**   AUGUST 11ᵀᴴ, DUSK. Tabulate them: your moments of fremitus, their causes variously grotesque, amorous, or wholly literary and vainglorious, and calculate the degree to which each has brought you near to a standstill of the heart.

See also **bucentaur, isopor, nucha, quicquidlibet**

froust

(fraʊst) [perhaps from *frowst*, 'armchair' or 'the stuffy air of a room lacking ventilation,' from *frowsty*, fusty or having an unpleasant smell, and from Old French *frouste*, ruinous or decayed] VERB

To luxuriate in stupefying heat.

(**1960** P. Z. WARLOW. *A History of Leisure*) **p 542** As in 1. the decadent frousting parlors of eighteenth century France, in those silken years before that Revolution which so swiftly guillotined aristocrats, melons, and frosted queens; such parlors offered floors of cushions with unimaginable springiness, as well as basins of whipped cream, the most technologically advanced (at the time) radiators to produce a heat feverish and toxic as the tropics, and ornamental ponds of coquettish fish. Of course, the great frousting parlors, including those enormous lounging vestibules of Versailles, were all burnt by the rebels led by the furiously nude figure of maiden Liberty. See also 2. the popular demi-jazz tune of our own mid-twentieth century, "Come Froust With Me," with all its toe-tapping smoothness.

See also **locutory, xenodochium**

fuligo

(fjus'laɪgəʊ) [taken directly from the Latin *fuligo*] NOUN

Soot.

(**1631**, C. TREWHELLA. *Vesuvius Triumphant*) **Act III, Scene iv.**

EPIMETHEUS: Welcome, friend, to this mine home.
Let not the ashes trouble thee; I do promise
In time, thou shalt come to see them as I may,
As the residue of dreams we ought not to have dreamed;
But not far have I explored such a thought.
Here be the window, glass melted long ago, here be the door
Half-buried in cinders, caught in seductive ajar,
Here be the dog which suffocated, and the petrified bread twice baked
The colonnade of knee-deep dust.
Here thou canst see! that mountain which appeareth now
so tranquil once again.
Now, the orchards be all skeletons, all eldritch arms,
All charcoal which doth thrive in devastation. Still do I swear it:
I vow to thee that these apples I mold myself are indeed as
delicious as any, my friend, any,
These apples I sculpt from my fistfuls of fuligo.

See also **kern**

garguill

(gɑ:gɪl) [Of unknown origin, but perhaps out of some error. Compare *gard* (from French *garde,* guard), the dewclaw of a boar] NOUN

The dewclaw of a stag.

(**1723** C. YSEULT. *Philosophia Oudenia,* revised edition) **p 241** And what is its function? Of this we know not. But the delicacy, the acuteness, the sheer bony vanity of the garguill all engender a sudden and transient philosophy based entirely upon the notion of purposelessness, and its excruciating excellence.

See also **abature, corbin, ycore**

gelatia

(dʒˌɛleɪʃ(ɪ)ə) [perhaps an etymologizing perversion (after Latin *gelāre* to freeze) of Latin *chălāzĭas*, hail, from Greek *chalaza*, χάλαζα, hail] NOUN

As written by John of Trevisa, in his 1398 translation of the proto-encyclopedia of Bartolomeus, De Proprietatibus Rerum*: "a whyte precyous stone shapen as a heyll stone, and it is so calde that it neuer hetith with fyre;" a hailstone.*

(**1723** A. CORNELIUS & J. T. ATHANASIA. *Treasures to be Catalogued and Possibly Destroyed*) **p 142** O'er desert dunes endless in repetition and paled by centuries of drought, past wand'ring corpses made unto paper by sun and past the autograph of the sidling snake, the soldiers return'd unto the red city with lips blue. Wrapt in mantles of black wool, e'en the warriors now home wept to see again the city dying each day for all the heat, and raised their hands with many fingers gone. Upon their journey unto the far northlands, where ice does groan in the form of vast cliffs and makes white isles where bears sail unto th' boreal lights, they did lose limbs and squires to the bite of the frost itself. Yet return'd now from their mission, they bore back victory: the greatest wealth of the gelatia, brought unto the royal court in a glory of ribbons and blessings of the morn. Summoning his legions, vessel of the godhead all studded with diamond, powdered in gold and holding ruby and moonstone 'neath invincible skin, the king demanded then the jewel, that he might cool his cheek e'en in midsummer's fever death. Yet within the soldiers' treasure-box, locked tight by a key swallowed by a gray colt killed in order to open it, there waited but a pool of waters clear and meaningless. For indeed the line twixt great fortunes and worthless things is but a clouds' veil easily rent, and of the hail-stone and the immortal gelatia, none could say what might more precious be.

See also **ætites, frazil, lygure, naricorn, pyrame**

halikeld

(hǝlɪˌkɛld) [from Old English *háliȝ*, holy + adapted Norse *kelda*, spring, well] NOUN

A sacred well.

(**1808** K. ISOM. *Widows I have known*) **p 119** When I knew Eveline—she with her hair like a steel loom, her eyes set within skeins of old skin, her nails tainted by seventy years' poisoning by quicksilver—long since had she withdrawn into her estate, ne'er venturing past the hedges clipped in animal forms and sleeping each night upon the peak of the western gable. Still wore she those ball-gowns with paper flowers decaying at the hem, exposing the clavicles broken by gray decades. Perhaps in loneliness or dementia's firm faith that she had known me once before, Eveline permitted me to stay in the servants' cramped quarters beneath the sweeping stair, all domestics having long since left, save for the taciturn and gnarled gardener with his necromantic shears. In the yellowing library, that purgatory between Shakespeare and rotted spine, she read repeatedly the same tempestuous adventures and regal tragedies, stunned once again by the catastrophic climaxes, gasping with the last revenants of her elegance; we dined at opposite ends of the banquet table still adorned with autumnal centerpieces, so far removed that I could scarce glimpse the quick gleam when she would pause to examine her own unfamiliar face mirrored in a tarnished spoon. When you were young, Eveline told me, you gathered the shattered sapphire shells of robins' eggs, and kissed the corpses of the embryonic infant birds. I would nod, and half believe, while the gardener tended the peonies growing wild and scarlet on their mound of packed earth. Eveline walked as does a duchess, through the labyrinth of lilacs and along the balcony where dithered the nameless and dour Persian cats, but recollected not her path or her own name. In retrospect, I suppose it was the halikeld—the well with its gaping granite mouth, its pail of holes, waiting there within the thicket of chipped, cherubic statuary— in which her last, most animate memories remained. One heard her mumbling gentle dialogues with the low resonances out of waters dark, echoes of great depth and drowned wings. Had I not departed for this city where life occurs in allegro and smog, I might glimpse Eveline still peering over the halikeld's treacherous brink, and perhaps suppose I could perceive in the subterraneous ripples a shining and breathless blue sphere, a form like the face of a small slumbering boy.

See also catacoustics

halit

(həlɪt) [adapted Latin *halit-us,* breath] NOUN

1. *An exhalation,* or, 2. *a perfume.*

(**1909** B. JOHANN. *The Survival*) **p 34** Upon my throat I bear my lover's breath, and within my breast, about my wrists, on my flawed scar. It is this fragile signature of skin, this illegible asterisk upon the sensory apparatus, this which signals and signs me as I step into a crowded, and yet hollow room, and when I walk in the dark. In the fare-thee-well of a curtain billowing in breeze the scent sweeps from the windowsill's iridescence of dead flies and along the crucial vanity of the bookcase and unto me. My lover's halit is the odor of sweat amidst the oleanders, and the nucleus of the snail's shell combed from the sea's treacherous green floor, of the secret bed, the journey and the temple of dragonflies—it is all her passions and helpless laughter, nightmares and confessions and pensive nights. It smells of her exhaling resuscitation into struggling lungs, of urgency and the mouth-to-mouth.

See also **myropolist**

hederated

('hɛdəreɪtɪd) [from Latin *hederāt-us*, crowned with ivy, (from *hedera*, ivy) + *-ed*, from Old English *–ede*, Old Saxon *–ôdi*, suffix denoting the possession of an attribute expressed by a noun] ADJECTIVE

Wearing a crown of ivy.

(**1711** R. F. GROVER. *An Old Woman in Norfolk, her distresses and how she solved them*) **p 94** When the old woman came to this place, with a train of black thread and an absence of memory, this was her favorite sight. Not the meadows from which came anonymous cries in the poppied afternoon, nor the broken columns shining and shadowed in the sallow winds,

nor even the pale horses drinking from the river's clouded mirror, which awoke in the old woman the sense that she had passed over the waters and come to those gardens they say will follow our deaths. What the old woman loved best was the spectacle of the hederated girl, moving there in the grove of spinal cypresses; she was tall and yellow of skin, and the old woman believed not that her bright toes ever touched the grasses beneath. Hands clasped and crumbling, the old woman would wait in the flushed evenings, rubbing her hunched back, 'til the appearance of that lovely wraith drifting slow amidst and through the trees. Sometimes the old woman called out a nonsense salutation, and once even brought forth an offering of bright barley gathered in her varicose arms. But never did the hederated maid respond. Still, the old woman minded it not. She came nonetheless to the grove upon each waning green dusk, settling in among the roots and rabbit skulls to wait for the vision of the girl's luculent wrists and that diadem of ivy: like a planet, like a riddle, like a familiar name.

See also **byss**

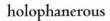
holophanerous

(hɒləʊˈfænərəs) [from Greek ὅλος, whole, entire + φανερός, manifest, wholly discernible] ADJECTIVE

Of insect metamorphosis, wholly discernable as complete.

(**1919** L. GRUFFYDD. *The Biology of Apprehension*) **p 359**
The existence of the non-holophanerous specimen seems
to Dr. Ecklebert to attest to the history of evolution as a
biography of increasing complexity.   Initially, the insect
seemed to be following the typical path of its biologic
order—oh! the lambent *Lepidoptera*—a path lined with
hormones coursing over the morphotectonic terrain of
shapeshifting: from pearly eggs unto wormhood, unto
larva, unto a pupa's somnambulism and the emergence
unto infinitely frail butterfly.   But the average insect's life
is indeed as fleeting as fish molded of marzipan, and after
the creature reaches a point of brief stasis Dr. Ecklebert
had expected it to fade into an empty husk of itself.   This

particular specimen, however, refuses to follow the universal law of evanescence. For as Dr. Ecklebert has monitored its growth, the thing has only continued in its transformation. Upon waxen wings, it has developed a sheen that defies the behavior of photons, with antennae now curled into the form of a cursive *e* which Ecklebert cannot pronounce, and a tongue extending to the length of the good doctor's own left arm. The butterfly is capable now of fluttering to the exhilarating altitude of hurricanes. It bites. It displays at this point two stomachs, abnormal lungs, and five incessant hearts; Dr. Ecklebert believes it to possess a primitive knowledge of mathematics. And it shows no signs of stopping. Though Ecklebert has always known that insect metamorphosis constitutes a minute and logical miracle, it fast grows physically impossible to bear the uncontrollable explosions of this specimen. Dr. Ecklebert awaits the next stage of the body's transformation, scarcely able to imagine what potential lies in that tiny and proportionately marvelous form.

See also **homœoteleuton, kermes, limax, xoanon, ycore, zumbador**

homœoteleuton

(həʊˌmiːəʊtɪ⟩l(j)uːtɒn)   [Latin, adapted Greek ὁμοιοτέλευτον, from ὅμοιος, like + τελευτή, end, ending] NOUN

The occurrence of identical endings in narratives or words.

(**1891** ROSEBLADE & GILFEATHER. *A Diary of Love among the Early Dead, and Childhood Lost*) **p 198** It is this which troubles me most of all. In the silver intuition of the night, I think of you and gain the distinct impression that all things are coming to their close. For do we not dance a fascinated and terrified dance with endings, to the tune of a tragedian's melodramatic breath? This you asked me once, I recall, and I answered you not. We rebel against the finish, you said, battling it with elixirs of hypothetical immortality and glittering cities intended to fight the eternal twilit failure of the day. Yet so too do we love conclusions; waiting for our books' endings to fall like the bridal veil of midnight, gasping at the pure satisfaction of all things tumbling into place—when each character shall stand where she must stand, impaled upon her fatal flaw, and each event shall come to its fiery apex, and each villain will lie draped in blood or silk. Let me tell the story of you and I: we the children upon a river, giggling at the infinitesimal sensuality of beetles scrambling over bellies and breasts; we hear now the tales told by the peacocks; I see the thrill, the awe, the awfulness of your throat; then there is a death, and so must I depart. Surely you recall the rest. And when all those filaments of narrative converge, you asked me once, is this not when we are happy at last? Yet here and now and blind as chance, I find myself perceiving that nothing before has ever been complete. I believe it quite possible that, in spite of childish hopes, all our tales were never in fact concluded. Rather all readers and rapt listeners and writers absconded, lovers who knew not their preciousness—we have enacted lives forever mouthing our anguished homœoteleutons, perched upon the cusp of a true and monstrous end: the journey by sea and the tempestuous isle, the hero with sword upraised, the doomed romances and the beds in the dusky fields have not yet found their resolution. You and I cannot be finished, not yet, not in this the ashen hour preceding an unexperienced dawn.

See also **chorizont, frantling, rifacimento, scytale, nucha, supernatant**

hyperalgic

(haɪpə(r)æl›dʒɪk) [representing Greek *hype*, ὑπερ, over, beyond, above measure + *algia*, αλγία, pain] ADJECTIVE

Possessing an abnormally sharp sensitivity to touch and pain.

(**1841** P. KIFFIN. *Disasters, or, Ella in Love*) **p 215** *I know
I feel things differently than the others do,* Euphemia once sighed,
perhaps unaware or perhaps hoping that somebody might
hear. Ella watched her forever from afar. And Euphemia
winced at the scratched sulfuric mockery of a lighted match,
her skin enduringly violet with bruises perpetual; *when I
come near to a candlestick,* she said, *I feel I shall die.* Never did
Ella dare take Euphemia's perpetually trembling hand, but
she did possess that valor to imagine how those clairvoyant
fingertips must surely have felt.

Hyperalgic Euphemia spoke aloud of her sensations,
in a high and desperate voice attempting to bring somebody,
anybody, to perceive the same tickling and agonies. *I can
sense the pressure of that pink kite overhead. A storm approaches; it is
like suffocation, or arriving fate.* Or, she would murmur, *I am
earth beneath a metropolis—there, I feel the bargaining and tumbling
oranges of the marketplace, and the weight of all homes sinking into me.
I feel the symbolism of sunlight,* she would say. *Raindrops destroy
me.*

To a butler: *my chair is bruising the thoughts of my thighs.*
Once, Ella glimpsed Euphemia rolling in terror upon the
garden's otherwise subtle grass, infatuated with the crickets'
shrill caress. A kiss and its profound consequences, Ella

supposed, would have been unbearable. But Euphemia could read the very heavens of *Paradise Lost* with her eyes shut, capable of distinguishing with her fingertips each angelic flourish of ink upon page. She wandered through atlases without a compass rose, lingering at the Himalayas in high relief, numbed ice temples with their frigid gods. A paper cut could send the girl to bed for weeks.

In some unprecedented circumstance, Ella dreamt, Euphemia could have sensed the lines of her palms as broken canyons, running deep with an unidentified heat, or might discern the footsteps of the fleas upon their skins, lending their nocturnal thoughts and disastrous gifts. But never did she venture to speak to her, not before Euphemia tore away her ashen hair—what this must have done to her—and flung herself into a bonfire: the experience unspeakable, unequivocal, unsurpassable and sanctified, ultimate death brought to ultimate reality. But just before her madness, Euphemia mouthed the only words she ever spoke to Ella, across a bridge like an appalled tongue: *I am very tired of the licks of my clothing, you know, and the summer will feel as love unwanted, yes, already I sense it, and then I shall be forced to endure the hands of the water hovering in the humid air. I'm really not a sensual person, deep down.*

See also **isopor**

idolum

(aıˌdəʊləm) [Latin *īdōlum*, adapted Greek *eidolon*, εἴδωλον, idol.] NOUN

1. *A specter*, or, 2. *an idea*, or, 3. *a fallacy*.

(**1799** FINNEGAN & MAHY, EDS. *Many Speculations upon the Fate of our Notions, revised anniversary edition*) **p 281** Certain philosophers, now exiled past the pale of the loony wastes, have ventured so far as to suggest that upon our deaths we shall all become idolums. They point to humanity's waxing quantities of all ideas to be possibly conceived, and its increasing load of idiot beliefs, an upsurge concurrent with our continuous processes of birth, dancing, and death. Indeed, simple numbers dictate that we shall all recur not as ghosts with hands, as we had assumed, but only as theories, as whims, as absurdities.

See also **lemure, spectrey**

i-hwat

(iːhwət) [Old English ȝehwæt, neuter of ȝehwá every one: = Old Low German gihvat, neuter of gihvê.] NOUN

Everything.

(**1919** G. W. WINDUS, ED. *Formulae of Being*) **p 313** In the kind of paradox that so entertains the crooked and

canny herons, *i-hwat* is not complete. For ought not there be an O? *ihowat,* or *ihwoat,* or *i-hwato,* or even perhaps *oi-hwat.* O, given the possibility of a round receptacle for all the sacred cows and irony and teaspoons, tabletops and mood swings, urine and daisies and metallurgy, plump figs and grandfather clocks, birds of prey and philosophers and blue pearls and pink sadness, volcanoes and non-Euclidian geometry and you and I and love—one would expect such a word to contain at least one O, oh, a hole to catch all these scraps of being within its hollow heart. But there is none. As such, one can draw a sequence of conclusions: firstly, *i-hwat* is everything. But *i-hwat* is imperfect. Thus, everything is imperfect.

See also **quicquidlibet, versipellous**

inquiline

(ˈɪnkwɪlaɪn) [adapted Latin *inquilīnus*, an indweller in a place not his own, a sojourner, lodger, from *in-*, Latin *intrāre*, inside + *colĕre*, to dwell. Compare French *inquilin*] ADJECTIVE, or, NOUN

1. *Dwelling in the nest of another species, or an animal which does so,* or, 2. *A sojourner.*

(**1810** D. BELLAPAIS. *The Clarity of the Miniscule Eye*) **p 26** She supposes that were she once again to reckon time in terms of her human cradle—relentless creature of literature, the grandfather clock, and the throat's woeful, winsome hyoid bone—it would seem not so long a time since she entered this place. But here in the beehive with its geometric atria and all the honey delectable and thick as seduction through and through, the minutes feel as eons would have to her childhood self, when her adept arms bore a dozen furious stings and she walked in wonder betwixt the irises; with prismatic and telescopic insect eyes she sees now too how wonderful was she, she with her dreaming wings. Here, she has nestled herself in amongst the bewildered infant bees, keenly aware of her body as once she was upon the incision of hominid skin and black blood and upon the moments of ecstasy. She believes the bees recognize her not, thinking her only a peculiar, altered or admirable worker in the meadows' world, or else know her as an alien but cherish her out of curiosity, sympathy, the enthrallment of the scientist's animal heart. Like all those who surround her she is lunatic for pollen, mad for the dusting of gold upon the infinitely delicate hinder leg, and like all of these her symmetric sisters she inhabits the perpetual, pulsating vision of the Queen. She is learning the language of the honeybees—a world written in dances, in improvised minuets— always has she been becoming what she is. Forever inquiline was she, and here she is, home, in the absolute, adamantine reality of the imagined life.

See also **corbicula, ziczac, zumbador**

interlucation

(ɪntərˈluːˈkeɪʃən) [adapted Latin (as mentioned in the works of Roman naturalist Pliny the Elder), *interlūcātiōn-em* (noun describing action from *interlūcāre,* from *inter,* between + *lux,* light, *lūc-em,* act of lighting] NOUN

The thinning of trees to allow the entrance of light.

(**1763** REDGEWELL & CREAK. *What happened in the forest*) **p 130** And nothing remained the same after the interlucation. Never before such a brilliance as this showed itself within the woods, the light now falling in columns and whorls and sanctified pools. Now the ferns whimpered under the new onslaught of sharpened dawn upon their tendrils, and with a groan finally unfurled spiraled fingers to drop their winsome spores and wither away. On the other hand, the wild strawberries sprawled with the inscrutable patterns of a child's solemn imagination, and the lupines flourished to a cathedral's height, and there was a veritable detonation of minute white daisies emitting a pollen like the dust of sinister confectioners. But concerning the people—woodsmen and huntresses, bandits and the mossy insane—never could they adapt to the change. At once, every flaw and freckle of one another's faces was revealed in a paradox of humiliated pleasure, and without the blanketing shadows a mid-afternoon nap became a maddening struggle with conscious dreams. Most terrifying of all was the sight of that great pale monitor moon, sweeping past Polaris and above them every night, peeking between the last of the bruised leaves to glimpse what the people were doing in their thriving beds.

See also **chiminage, dendrolatous, diatyposis, nemoral, nervure, porraceous, rampick**

isabelline

(ɪzə›bɛlɪn) [from the feminine name *Isabella*, though the origin of the adjective remains uncertain] NOUN, or, ADJECTIVE

Yellow-gray.

(**1940** F. SELBY-UPSHELL. *The Innocent Birthday*) **p 126** Her delight rendered Ebenezer's effort entirely worthwhile, in spite of the drudgery. Most children are fairly easy to surprise, wearing for at least their first decade the tiaras of the present moment and existence-in-it. But Ebenezer's daughter was more prescient than that, with the quick astuteness of enormous eye that guessed at all the machinations of arithmetic and of grown-ups; one could see, at each birthday and desperately extravagant holiday, the manner in which she merely feigned astonishment at every gift. This time, however, Ebenezer did believe that he had devised a true surprise, and though the task was backbreaking, he managed to keep it a secret. But what labor! beginning first with the crayon companies, the elite arthouses of youth. It required a dedicated campaign of letters and sycophantic scrapings to convince them to fabricate for him the new color. Subsequently Ebenezer herded together the painters, the realists and the absentminded impressionists. He begged them, wooed them with baskets of mulberry muffins until finally they agreed to incorporate the girl's namesake hue into their works, particularly those images of foxes (the child had vulpine predilections). With pocket change and notes of immortal debt he paid off the encyclopedists to tint the historical photographs of Turkish princesses. By this time, the strain of his efforts had left him sore and stricken with terrible migraines, during which Ebenezer had slimy visions of the color itself. Most difficult of all was the tyrannical rainbow itself—and how impudent, how imprudent he was to attempt to persuade the spectrum which normally deigns to speak to crystals alone—and how profoundly he spoke, kneeling in the teardrops of a rain shower's remains. And light itself, electromagnetic physics feeling merciful or impassive or curious, at last acquiesced. Prior to Ebenezer's endeavors, such a tone had appeared nowhere, not in the prescient prisms, not in cumulonimbus or in pigment, in Saturn or a bubble's skin, not in the exuberant spray of the sprinkler system, not in the hide of a vanishing antelope— no, its appearance was his doing entirely. But now, isabelline existed. And Ebenezer could proudly state that the child was indeed surprised, and pleased to the point of helpless laughter, and all his toil was made meaningful to see Isabella's delight.

See also **coquelicot, heliotrope, porraceous, watchet, xanthopsia**

isopor

(aɪsəʊpɔː)   [from Greek *isos*, *ἴσος*, equal + *poros*, *πόρ-ος*, passageway] NOUN

A line (either imaginary or on a map) connecting points at which equal changes in some parameter of the earth's magnetic field are observed.

(**1841** P. KIFFIN. *Disasters, or, Ella in Love*) **p 254** It is a fact, scientifically proven and personally disquieting, that the planet's magnetic poles oscillate in place and power over the course of the eons; this presents a great problem for the romantic. And Ella fell in love like a lost mariner, so that each potential amour presented itself to her as a lush and morally ambiguous landfall, tormenting the far reaches of her vision, but upon consulting the temperamental compass she could never locate the one for whom she yearned. Configurations would change, so that Ella detected one lover to be waiting lachrymose upon a white shore where stones sliced one's feet deep enough to release a bluebird blood, but upon arriving at that barren coast found that whatever force had drawn her to that mournful woman—and indeed, there she stood— had once again shifted entirely. She followed her isopor then to a mountaintop upon which one could no longer believe in the existence of the earth, but the man she found here possessed hands of a different polarity, and so was she dragged away, somewhere towards the Dog Star prancing across the southern sky. The compass giddied itself unto the Silk Road, and Ella journeyed to a bastion of bougainvillea in a nation where heat was measured not in degrees but in quantity of blooms. But this lover wore not a single anklet as had been expected, and so was Ella already tugged again towards the tinkling of another metal entirely. Magnets attract, and they repel; the Arctic and the Antarctic express their love in an enticement impossible to redeem and yet too electrifying to bear; the aurora swung forth and back and sang duets over Ella's feverish head. And it was one possible lover, a woman who dwelt so far south as to live half in handstand, with skin become green as the libertine leeks, who suggested to Ella's receding footsteps that the girl had always been truly in love with the force itself, as the forlorn albatross journeying towards the lights over a boundless sea.

See also **canicular, cosmognosis, fremitus, hyperalgic, quicquidlibet**

jargonelle

(dʒɑːgəˌnɛl) [adopted French *jargonelle*, a very gritty variety of pear, diminutive of *jargon*, a colorless, smokeless variety of the mineral zircon found in Sri Lanka, apparently itself derived from Arabic *zarqūn*] NOUN

An early-ripening pear.

(**1758** P. O'MOHEN. *Poor poems for the peckish*)

> Beware, my boy, the jargonelle, with its encardion of fright
> Beware the jewel seeds, the speckled skin of spite—
> For though the flesh be honey and the orchard seems a prance
> It proveth true that all our sweets are but a cruel romance.
> Awaken when the dawn stoppeth all the things that be
> Look up! The crop doth sink with nasty juice in circles about thee.
> And shouldst thou find thyself entrapp'd by shock of early pear
> Thou hast much eating left to do, wouldst thou escape from there.

See also **encardion, tribuloid**

jornada

(dʒɔːˈnɑdə) [Spanish *xorˈnaðǎ* = Italian *giornata*, French *journée*, literally 'a day's space, work, or journey'; in Spanish also 'an act in a Comedy'] NOUN

1. *An act of a play,* or, 2. *a long day's journey made without water.*

(**1758** M. DE LA VEGA, TRANSLATED S. OLDERSHAW. *How our voyage does not end, or, The Tragedy of the Desert, or, El Infinidad*) **p 726** We remain uncertain of how long the jornada has been. We know that we have been in near-constant motion, and we know that the radiance does not cease. Life—as much as it continues to be—is all tarantella of shifting lights, a particular, thunderous violet which falls upon our faces when we become disheartened, a red glow that strikes our bodies when occasionally we cannot help but collapse, and at times a harsh pillar of light that trains upon a single one of us like the focused surveillance of the sun. We think that we are seen, but we know too we cannot hide. We are watched, and it is expected, scripted, unavoidable: we must move on, and on, and forever on. Indeed, as some of us have agreed in flat whispers, it seems at times that our steps and gesticulations have been carried out before, and shall again by others more mortal than we. At times, the sky is so evocative that we are willing to believe any story, but rarely can we discern what happens in the dark before us and behind. We do not know why we wear these absurd gowns, or why our seraphic swords are but blades of wood which kill us not, even as we are so desperate to stop. But yet of all our deliberate gestures and the weight of our false jewels, it is our throats that torment us most. For we find that we are speaking always, shouting significance and chanting futile spells and professing with too-blatant passion these lines whose meaning escapes us. At times, some of us insist that this poetry is anything but new and our art is mimicry, and does not bear our names. We are echoes, they say, echoes of roles enacted many times before; our words are not our own. We have spoken, danced in elegy, cried out for so long that our throats carvings in serpents' sands. Anything, anything for a broken glass of water—but we can only move on, and on, and on, in these repetitious steps and signs. What shall become of us without the mercy of drink? One of us has said, and will say again, that of all moments the instant of relieved thirst is the most sublime and cataleptic. Without it, we know that soon enough our voices will be incapable of amplification, growing inaudible and inarticulate and meaningless as words; we will speak only to ourselves. The lights scorch us. We believe that we are seen; we only hope that we are heard.

See also **catacoustics**, **rifacimento**, **wlonk**

jumelle

(dʒuːˌ›mɛl) [adapted French noun and adjective (feminine noun; masculine *jumeau*), doublet of *gemelle* or *gemeau*, from Latin *gemellus*, diminutive of *geminus*, twin. Formerly naturalized; now an alien French word.] NOUN

I. *Anything consisting of something twinned or in a pair, or, 2. a pair of opera glasses.*

(**1839** SALLOWAY, BUNTING, & DILKS. *The Music of Inconvenience*) **p 220** One quality of any bilateral, bipartite thing proves to be the compulsive capacity to replicate itself. The two sides of the object in question divide to generate their own counterparts, with the perilous art imparted by proportion, and thusly do these mirrored offspring themselves divide to perpetuate the course. Through warped microscope we see the amoebae in heat participating in this grand tradition, as do certain other things. Thus it was in 1732 that the dilemma of the jumelles came to its own skillful culmination. Partially one could blame the contemporaneous fashion of opera— the epic tragedies accentuated by phenomenal hats, suicidal violins, vocal cords more anguished than those of the amorous nightingales. Palatial auditoriums arose, featuring beehives of balconies so lofty that elderly spectators and women imprisoned in corsets would faint in the thin altitudinous air. Also requisite, then, were delicate golden binoculars, the lovely jumelles that would permit one to glimpse each pore of the soprano's painted face as her heart snapped, and each dyed hair of the tenor raising his hands to an artificial meteor. As any good inventor knows, 'tis symmetry that pleases most the aesthetic of the well-trained gaze, one golden eyepiece alongside another. What was not anticipated, however, was the sudden outbreak of self-fracturing duplication among the jumelles, so that Europe at once found itself overrun by jubilant pairs of opera glasses, spreading with a speed that no epidemic had possessed since the rosy rhymes of the bubonic plague. Indeed, it took a full two years to eradicate those aristocratic bacteria, the constantly dividing and generating and spying pests.

See also **wlonk**

kantikoy

(ˈkæntɪkɔɪ) [taken from the Algonquin] VERB

To dance in worship, celebration, or in honor of the dead.

(**1888** C. WITHERBY & L. HUWS. *Spirituality of the Miniscule*) **p 161**   How peculiar, that the flies should take part in the kantikoy after so many millennia of mutation and invasion; yes, after vexing the ancestors of the ancestors of the progenitors across every continent—save Antarctica and the eighth landmass which has long since floated away—how strange that they should adopt the kantikoy. Then again, we ourselves have stolen weeping life and verdant territory and lilting words, so perhaps such learned virulence is not an isolated event.   In our lessons of hygiene, of organism and microorganism, we have learnt to despise the buzzing of the order *Diptera*, reading them as signals of filth and pandemic. Then again, we have brought our own diseases. But we have devised a bitter spectrum of repellents: some daub the carnivorous fat of lions on the brow, or bury wolves' tails in their walls, or swat or spray or douse themselves in poison merely to move a wingspan away from the prismatic eye. Still there exists a certain sacrosanct side to the flies, which we confess that in spite of frankincense and flagellation so many of us have failed to achieve. In the windswept isles off the lonesome Scottish coast, there are certain flies who do not die, and in some blazing summers infestations of brass flies arise from southern sewers. In ancient Rome Pliny writes that concoctions of nuts, breastmilk, ashes, and flies' heads will cure our lunar baldness. And in spite of pestilence, all flies are mystics of a godless piety, in their fascination with our food and our feces and our corpses. For communing upon the unexpected treasure of our excrement, the insects enact their compulsive and stilted dance, rubbing foreleg to creeping foreleg, adulating matter's secret and ceaseless metamorphosis in the fantastical gut.

See also **kermes, inquiline, limax, xoanon**

kae

(ke) [Northern form of Middle English *co*, corresponding to Middle Duutch *ca*, *ka(e*, Old High German *chaha*, *châ* (Middle High German *kâ*), Danish *kaa*, Norwegian *kaae*. The direct source may have been an Old Norse **ká*, *k*; or, onomatopoeic]

NOUN I. *A jackdaw's cry*, or, 2. *A jackdaw itself*, or, ADJECTIVE 3. *Clever*.

(1747 Z. PROTHERA & E.M.BAYLEAF. *Chronicles of the Avian Wars*, volume VII) **p 757** Observation has shown the jackdaw to be capable of tying and undoing even a mariner's impossible knots, of recognizing its own glinting beak in the mantles of green pools, and scratching out rudimentary verbs with its unscrupulous claws. Indeed, there is reason to believe that the word *kae* itself was invented by the jackdaws, a particularly cunning play on their part.

See also **chirm, engastration, shiterow**

kermes

(ˈkɜːmɪz) [adopted French *kermès*, Italian *chermes*, Spanish *carmes*, Portugeuse *kermes*, adapted Arabic and Persian *qirmiz* (whence came also adjectives *carmine, cramoisy, crimson*)] NOUN, or, ADJECTIVE

1. *The pregnant female of the insect* Coccus ilicis, *formerly believed to be a berry; gathered in large quantities for use in dyeing and formerly in medicine,* or, 2. *the species of evergreen oak,* Quercus coccifera, *upon which it dwells and feeds,* or, 3. *the red dye-stuff consisting of the dried bodies of these insects,* or, 4. *bearing a likewise red hue.*

(**1899** C. WITHERBY & V. HAWKES. *Tragedies of the Infinitesimal*) **p 83**   Let us follow now the miniscule biography of Arabella, the beetle who at her largest was approximately the size of an ostrich's paranoid eye, the queen who reached approximately seven months in age, the lone lover who was sexually linked to the North Star—the kermes who was not aware of memory. An entomologist with tendencies of personification may consider Arabella a reasonably happy being, when she dwelt for the sunlit span between two equinoxes in a desiccated desert oak, after her birth amidst a stellar cluster of eggs laid by an anonymous hermaphrodite. Like most of her five hundred siblings, Arabella emerged with visions of a pearlescent city in flames, and her soft, bulbous body shone with the luculent hue of pus. Thrice did her flesh exceed its skin, and thrice she split and shed it, leaving behind a trail of husks as specters of herself. Passing from the innocent larval stage, she embedded herself within chewed wood to dream again of that pale metropolis ablaze; awakening with a new solidity of lustrous exoskeleton, she emerged from her cell to heed the parallel whisperings of the oak and her own skittering, brittle legs. Though she viewed them not, the underside of her fanned wings bore the image of a broken sphinx. Content was Arabella to sense only the motion of thunderheads over a windswept continent, till upon her seventh full moon trembled at once with an unexpected Darwinian lust, which she sated with her own multifarious genitalia. And then did she die, crush at the hands of a species for whom transience is equated oft to insignificant. Yet what Arabella realized not—though perhaps it is the case that insects do possess an elegant astronomy all their own—was the beloved thing her living corpse had forever been. Gathered by graverobbing wayfarers, pulverized by mute slaves, she was a paste to be daubed upon a pharaoh's feline eyes; she was the stuff of fabulous elixirs, administered alchemically to aristocrats vomiting in a delirium of towers collapsing unto ash.

She was the plunder given in submission to the geometrical armies of ravenous Rome, ransacked mandibles, and she was the tincture of the soldiers' crimson plumes. Her cadaver became the painted mouth of criminal angels in frescoes believed to save the soul, and all was to be paid in wounds. But never could Arabella have known what her body might come to be, all for the sake of red.

See also **coquelicot, kantikoy, limax, xoanon**

kirn

(kɜ:n) [Verb 'to churn' from Scottish dialect, likely from Old Norse *kirna*, to churn; other senses of uncertain etymology; perhaps of more recent origin, or from Old English ʒ*e-cyrn*, meaning uncertain, but related to Old High German *gilkurni*, denoting corn (before arrival in England of New World maize, used to describe any grain) collectively or of all kinds; ʒ*e-cyrn* may perhaps have been a noun establishing the completion of the reaping-time] VERB, or, NOUN

1. *To churn*, or, 2. *the act of the harvesting of the last handful of corn*, or, 3. *the harvest festival*, or, 4. *a mire*.

(**1705** SCHEMBRI, LEONARD, & SIMCOX. *Almanack of the Peasants and their cats*) **p 148** And as twilight tumbles o'er the fields, its burden too vast now to rest any longer upon the anxious scaffolds of the evening stars, the people pluck that last handful—that kirn, that yepsen, that preciousness—of the earth's golden charity, and boil't in a cheery pot to eat as one eats a well-told tale, churning the milk till there emerges the butter like a spirit summoned, like a healing wound. And the dance begins, in circles and in garlands and in blooms, and their song is a ribbon unraveling all the clothes so torn with the daily toil of summers past.   Onward spins the dance, till the moon is cajoled to hop upon one round paw, and thence do join the bats with their peculiar twittering jig. And by that hour when day breaks itself an egg o'er the harvesters exhausted and a-slumber in a drunken heap, the field trodden lies unto a bog, wholly a swamp of fruit and melodies in mud, lost shoes and ten thousand footprints o'er all the possible harvest of the year to come.

See also **yepsen**

latitant

('lætɪtənt) [adapted Latin *latitant-em*, present participle of *latitāre*, to lie hidden; first appearing 1646, Sir Thomas Browne's *Pseudoxia Epidemica*, to describe 'lizards, snakes, and other divers insects'; later expanding to include 'magicall powers,' bubbles of air, heretics, and those who wear makeup] ADJECTIVE, or, NOUN

1. *Hiding, as in refuge or in wait of ambush*, or, 2. *that which hides or is latent.*

(**1660** THE WRIT OF BANDOGS, ET AL. *Warnings for the King, in times of assassination and revolt*) **p 24** Your Majesty, take heed: beneath thine sin'ster bed, as is traditional; within the lilacs (not in the hedges, but in the minute and horrendous blossoms themselves); on the other side of the throne; behind (and also inside) the painting of the bathing nymph upon the western wall; open-mouthed in the jars of candied ginger and, aye, pots of shimm'ring paint to be daubed upon a cheek; in the cobblestones' cracks, hoping to snatch at thine unknowing footsteps; oft'times in the cupboard, with teeth; pressed blackletter 'tween the pages of the dictionary, awaiting thine eye all a-shiver; also curled within the an onion's cosmic core.

See also **encardion, tremogram**

lecithal

('lɛsɪθəl) [from Greek λέκιθ-ος, yolk] ADJECTIVE

A word utilized to describe those egg cells possessing a yolk.

(**1784** M. HUMPHREY HAVERSHAM. *A Strange Occurrence in the Night-Time*) **p 55** One of the most startling experiences of his life would forever remain the eve when, with a mammalian yelp, he discovered beneath the pillow a magnificently yellow and inexplicable ball of raw slime; he understood that he himself may or may not have been the one to deposit the yolk within the wraiths' nests and sleepwalking brunches wherein dines the slumbering mind, laying eggs in a lecithal nightmare he could not recall.

See also **nyctograph, pheal**

lemniscus

(lɛmˈnɪskəs)   [adapted Latin *lēmniscus*, a ribbon, Greek λημνίσκος] NOUN

1. *the division symbol* ÷*, or,* 2. *the sign* ÷ *used by ancient textual critics in their annotations, or,* 3. *a minute ribbon-like appendage in the generative pores of some entozoans, or,* 4. *a closed curve as a figure 8, or,* 5. *A bundle of fibres in the central nervous system, especially those connecting sensory nuclei to the brain.*

(**1774** O. WHITFIRE. *The Unread Tome*) **p I**   Now do I hold in broken hand the lemniscus; this is its absolute lightness, insubstantial a notion and intricate as the fingerprint. This is its symmetry, and this is how it is within me. And as Sir Thomas Browne informed me, one hundred improbable years ago, *studious observers may discover more analogies in the book of nature, and cannot escape the elegancy of her hand.* Yes, certain structures recur and names repeat, thoughts reappearing in a new body only to depart, and the words reinvent themselves only to rupture against the substance of the world, and the story must happen to us all over again.

See also **catacoustics, virgula**

lemures

('liːmə(r)ːz) [adapted Latin *lemures*, singular *lemur* (mythology)]

1. *as named by eighteenth century naturalist Carolus Linnaeus, genus of nocturnal primates of the family* Lemuridæ, *found chiefly in Madagascar; animals of this genus,* or, 2. *the spirits of the dead.*

(1799   FINNEGAN & MAHY, EDS.   *Many Speculations upon the Fate of our Notions, revised anniversary edition*) **p 309** Pattering silent upon paws which might be exquisite—if only visible to diurnal sight—they slip past the mosquito net fragile as a christening veil. The slumberer twisted in fever sheets perceives them only with the selective oracular ocular power bestowed by a dream, but awakens for but a moment with no more than a slight caress of dread, and returns to the vision of lost love. And they climb then into the cupboards, playing dirges with teaspoons tapped to chime upon porcelain plates, and they examine the flour to imagine the sheer pleasure of mortal bread. In disquieted sleep we pluck at the air as if in search of mandolin; they attend to our woeful murmurs with terrified curiosity, bound away. They swing from the palm rafters and chitter unknown wisdom or idiocy to the weepy moon, leaking through windows left open to the tropic heat and staining with pearl the earthen floor. Panting slightly, extending tiny tasteless tongues, they scrutinize the artifacts of our lives: the fascinating glint of a pocketknife, a rubber ball, marvelous ribbons and waterlogged books whose purpose they do not recall. We wake to the wail of the bird-of-paradise and the distinct saccharine scent of coconut rotted before dawn, believing for a moment we can discern in shadow the gleam of enormous, shocked, familiar eyes.

See also **idolum, spectrey**

levigate

('lɛvɪgeɪt) [from Latin *lēvigāre*, from *lēvis*, smooth.] VERB

To smooth, burnish, grind, or polish, bringing to a state of extreme shininess or to a fine powder.

(**1855** J. VOYLE. *How To Avoid Fame with Grace and Plentiful Style: A Manual*) **p 156** Theodoric the Levitator is admittedly a marvel. Certain, one cannot deny the astonishing and efficient manner in which he drifts nine inches above the floor, floating across the stage and juggling live kittens while his sparkling telekinetic globes spin in midair. Congratulations are indeed due to Theodoric the Levitator for his achievement of the International Magician's Tremendous Excellency Prize. But one ought not to neglect the work of Archibald the Levigator, who while perhaps not so ostentatious as the famed Theodoric nonetheless performs marvels of his own. See Archibald the Levigator burnish a teapot to unimaginable brightness and proceed to signal a hawk with its shine! See him grind a lump of whalebone to dust and sprinkle it as sugar upon his waffles. Archibald the Levigator can make even a tree's rotting stump glint like star-snot, and he can polish silverware until not even potatoes and gravy can stifle its gleam. Archibald the Levigator has buffed and waxed the spoons of the deposed royal families of Europe, and he can lend a patina to a donkey's belly, and not even Theodoric can say that.

See also **pantler**

libeccio

(lɪˈbɛtʃəʊ) [adopted Italian, from Latin *lib-s*, the south-west]
NOUN

A southwest wind.

(**1765** M. CARPANINI. *Voyage of the Good Ship* Eventide Bird) **p 490** From the Arabs with their astrolabes of zodiac gold, the Captain came to recognize the ways of the eastern wind. Aye, he told the mate, 'tis a crimson current driven wholly by the dreadful melody of morn. Well might the crew have rose in mutiny, when the Captain tossed the compass to the mouths of the frolicsome sharks, and declared them the galleon of the purposeful lost. But too charmed a figure was he, in his five-cornered hat with its tropical plumes, growing more melancholic according to the proximity of the ghostly green shore and more like a favorite uncle as he plotted their course towards oblivion. Trust thyself to wind, he declared. By way of offshore alchemy, he said, I know the northern storm, the air bearing the rooks upon whose claws the ice crystals ride reckless. From attacks of inopportune romanticism, I have come to understand the libertine tempests of the south, pilgrims come to teach their equatorial ways. Moreover there are the breezes of north-northwest, smelling of invisible ink, and the northeastern air incurring in stowaways a kind of rheumatic fear. But, the Captain sighed—exhalation being the wind's vanity mirror—but, my mates, I find myself craving most the libeccio: mezzo-soprano, if you too can hear it, there, and a little too forceful and a little too wry. This is why we steer such a course as now we do, away and ever away. Let fly the map! Turn the spyglass to the stars! Let fly the sails! Let fly my illustrious hat!

See also **anachorism, ythe**

limax

('laɪmæks) [Latin *līmāx*, a snail or slug] NOUN

A slug.

(**1846** Q. E. S. LENAHAN. *Suggestions for the Beginning Poet*) **p 50** The insecto-sexual rhymes inherent in this word make it a particularly juicy candidate for racy entomological poetry.

See also **holophanerous, kermes, xoanon**

locutory

(ˈlɒkjʊtərɪ)   [adapted medieval Latin *locūtōri-um*, from *locūtor*, one who speaks + *-ory*, suffix from Old English *orie* and Latin *ōria*, denoting a place or an instrument] NOUN

A room set aside (originally in a monastery) for the purposes of conversation.

(**1894** A. MacORIAGHTY. *A Great Many Questions Unanswered, and Mysterious Mysteries, which may entertain the curious or logical Reader*) **p 291** The detectives were baffled entirely by the locutory murders, frustrated till they wept tears of tweed into meerschaum pipes. It wasn't even that the locutory murders were particularly gruesome (unlike the library vivisections) or audaciously inventive (unlike the burglar marmosets with diamonds glinting on their ambidextrous toes). It was their sheer bloodless inexplicability; it is not every day that a city's morgue must contend with a dozen identically open-mouthed corpses, or that a team of constables must enter a room so scattered with cups of unfinished tea and the empty offerings of lifeless hands, and moreover so bereft of clues. For the chamber in which the corpses were found—this being the sumptuous locutory of the discreetly unscrupulous mansion of silver eaves and sterling flowerbeds lolling at the edge of town and of imagination—bore no directly incriminating or even inspirational evidence. Indeed, the door was barred from within, and the window impeccable, unbroken, insolently scenic. The twelve dead (two librarians, seven ancestrally wealthy dilettantes, a mildly talented painter, a baker (already butchered) and the obligatory candlestick-maker) slumped with seeming comfort in armchairs velveteen, and were stained by neither gore nor arsenic's limy drips. No disembodied heart pounded beneath the floorboards as a messy tattletale. And in their offices the detectives cursed for hours upon redundant hours, pounding fists upon tables and impugning one another's deductive skill. None could determine what horror could have transpired in that chamber of talkative luxury, until someone suggested the classic method of the adder, slipped in through a ventilation shaft. But, the others argued, homicide by snakebite is a desperate cliché, at which point someone else complained of that mounting peril of deathly boredom, and everything became all too clear.

See also **froust, xenodochium**

lygure

(lɪgjʊə(r)) [also appears as *lugre*, *ligurie*, or erroneously *ligerios*; adapted from Latin *ligūrius*, adapted Greek λιγύριον, apparently a variant of a word which appears in many different forms, as λαγούριον, λιγγούριον, λιγκούριον; the last of these (adopted in late Latin as *lyncūrius*) is connected with Greek λαγκ-, lynx, + οὖρον urine. The word may conceivably have some distant connection with the source of *azure* and *lazuli*.]
NOUN

A fabled gemstone formed from the concretion of lynx urine.

(**1723** A. CORNELIUS & J. T. ATHANASIA. *Treasures to be Catalogued and Possibly Destroyed*) **p 134** The powers of the lygure are much exalted— we are told that it is a Wish-Granter, more steadfast than the glittering godmothers, who at any rate are largely all sots. Claim the wise, with the aid of a lygure all that one desires shall flitter into life as the snowflakes arrive upon the tip of an extended tongue. Moreover, the dandy of good taste might well enjoy a lygure to be worn about the toe. But our age, we find, is one not only of delightful illumination but also of subterranean treachery, and so must we guard against the false lygures proliferating in our lavish marketplaces. The apothecary, cloaked in well-spoken shades of heliotrope, assures us that the lygure he offers is as authentic as his own mother, and perhaps represents the urine of a particular lynx of nobler ancestry than its counterparts. But one must not be fooled, for one is as likely to find an ersatz gem as one is to catch a digestive ague. The counterfeit lygures are most often formed of charcoal and pear juice, or otherwise the piss of mangy alleyway cats, those scraggly tiberts with their musical paws. And what consequence be such a sham? A spurious lygure in fact shall confer the opposite of that which one covets—should one wish for a beautiful mole upon the cheek, one receives a fern-shaped freckle upon the rump; should one ask for mounds of gold, one descends into the glamour of absolute tatter-shod poverty. A man who seeks sweets shall receive barrels of turmeric, and a woman who demands a mansion shall find herself bound to the prow of a white ship. Most devious of all, the false lygure shall convince one that such deception was what was desired all along, and that by virtue of this devious generosity, one is happy now.

See also **ætites, fernticle, gelatia, naricorn, tibert**

mamuque

(mæ›mʊk) [From post-classical Latin *Mamuco Diata*; in the January 1523 Cologne edition of Maximilian of Transylvania's account of the circumnavigation of the world, named as *De Moluccis*; in the November 1523 Rome edition, named *Manuccodiata*, from the Javanese word, *manuk déwâtâ*, from *manuk* bird + *déwâtâ*, male deities collectively] NOUN

A fabulous, wingless bird which feeds upon the air, founded upon erroneous accounts of the bird of paradise.

(**1533** ANONYMOUS. *Bestiarium Maestitia*) **p 17** Patient be the Mamuque, for it singeth not beneath the torment

of Sun or tyrant Saturn, nor doth it Flie as is Naturall to the Birds and their Warriors. Nay, the Mamuque doth only writhe in Silence upon the Earth, through forests where e'en the Slav'ring Science of the Wolves shall know it not, and it feasteth only upon the barren Aer and the Songs which float upon't. So do we catch its Gasps from the wild wold, its wretch'd Sighs and many Moans, and name the Mamuque a Lowly Beaste. But this order be but tempor'y. For there will come a Tyme when all the Grasse shall become but blades of Wind, and all Trees shall be as ash, and so shall the waves upon the Sea turn still. All the Animals shall curl togedare in a bed and die in sorrow, and the people shall starve unto Nothing. But upon our demise then shall the Mamuque ascend with much Feather'd Pleasure to the Reign it hath awaited, for in the Court of the Desolate the sole Emp'ror shall be that Bird who needeth naught, save the whisp'ring Aer.

See also **amphisbaena**, **barghest**, **bucentaur**, **dipsas**, **disomus**, **pyrausta**, **scytale**, **urisk**, **wasserman**, **yale**, **ythe**

morbidezza

(ˌmɔːbɪˈdɛtsə) [from Italian *morbidezza*, softness, delicacy, nonchalant grace, (of women and children) a delicacy of complexion (14th century), or softness of tonality or harmony of light and shade in a painting, harmony of proportions in a statue or relief (16th century), from *morbido*, morbid + *-ezza* (*-ess*), suffix delineating nouns of quality] NOUN

1. *An extreme softness and fragility,* or, 2. *A technique in painting creating lifelike and delicate images of flesh,* or, 3. *a smoothness and softness in music.*

1876   L. CAVENDISH-JANES.   *Transformations to be Emulated, in the Interest of Being Interesting*) **p 105**   But morbidezza is more than that. Morbidezza refers also to the passionate dance which in 1777 swept across thousands of verandas of stylish, sinful, sultry, starlit youth; it was once the most *au courant* of activities, with jerking hips and opened, saccharine mouths, quivering in ¾ time. They did the morbidezza. And morbidezza represents also a particular species of eastern European spider, with a sundial belly and venom excreted in precise dosages at the tip of each pinprick leg. Incidentally, the morbidezza lays its eggs in umbrellas left folded and obsolescent by the door. Morbidezza is that delicate aesthetic technique that renders dangerously believable the existence of a fallen, lustful angel in a banned painting. It was also the name of a certain village on the Adriatic coast which traded solely in the invisible ink of invisible cuttlefish, until that sultry day when at last the sea swallowed Morbidezza. *Morbidezza* was an anonymously composed and nearly inaudible symphony of the seventeenth century, which has not been performed since the Revolution. Morbidezza is a special type of scarf, woven with alarmingly intricate configurations of imaginary paisleys and historically worn as the kerchief of spies. Morbidezza is the name of somebody the reader once knew. Morbidezza is more than that—it is a disease of the skin, and it is a many-eyed monster of myth; morbidezza is a philosophy, and morbidezza is a lethal dessert.

See also **noyade, telarian**

motatorious

(məʊtəˌtɔərɪəs) [post-classical Latin *motatorius,* given as insect epithet in 1758 by naturalist Carolus Linnaeus, *Systema Naturæ*; post-classical Latin *motator,* mover; classical Latin *mōtāre,* + *ous,* from Latin *ōsus, suffix* denoting 'full of, abounding in'] ADJECTIVE

Vibratory or in a constant motion, as in the appendages of some insects.

(**1894** H. PEAGRAM. *A Marriage of True Binds*) **p 159** Edna adopted the skill with the sole objective of irritating Elbert; after sixty years, his habits vexed her to such a magnitude so as to tint her fingernails with the sullen copper of unexpressed wrath. Edna despised how Elbert would suck on his apricots for hours at a time, until the cloying flesh had dissolved in drips of pulp over his yellowed beard, and left him an elaborate, poisonous pit. She hated that he kept those pits, too, and his musty odor, a miasma like those ghouls which dwell in damp cellars. Thus did she kneel amidst the naïve daisies, despite stiffened hips and doorknob knees, and apprenticed herself to the crickets in their black metropolis. At last came the melodically still night of her revenge. Elbert jolted from sleep with a befuddled shout, to the din of his wife's wrinkled legs, shrill and stubborn and marvelously unpleasant. He flung pillows and pepperpots, but to no avail (prudently, Edna had learnt also the entomological leap). So filthily did he curse as to spoil the goats' milk, but joyful Edna only continued her deafening song. Not to be browbeaten, Elbert soon found a weapon of his own.

Most fortuitously, the fidelity of sun and earth dictated that this particular August should mark the seventeenth year of the cicadas' slumber in the muted dirt. Having taken up the glory of the virago, the insects awoke to hum strident lectures amidst the drooping apricot trees. Elbert clambered up into nectar and bough, where after cursory observation he began to vibrate with an earsplitting and thigh-rending drone. Edna only amplified herself, as she had long ago learnt to do. Perhaps the two would have trilled their bitterness for yet another decade, if not for the torrential thunderstorm and poor horoscope of another continent, which spurred the plague of migratory locusts. When the tiny green beings descended, collapsing the shed and blinding the Dog Star and decimating the orchard with a screaming buzz, the two could do naught but retreat into the house. Their windowpanes cracked, and their last teeth rattled sourly, and little corpses tumbled down the chimney in spirals of frantic ash. Edna and Elbert continued rubbing their hands and bony feet, decrepit thighs and bellies of dust, hoping to salvage the disaster by annoying one another to no end. In the close quarters of the kitchen, they quivered with a unified and rather familiar screech in concordant discord with the pandemonium of insect legs. Edna and Elbert felt a bit sentimental then, for the motatorious song of the locusts is at times a battle cry, but at others a mating call.

See also **rheotaxis**

mulligrubs

(ˈmʌlɪgrʌb) [origin uncertain; perhaps related to Middle French *megrim*, a migraine, vertigo, melancholy, or a whim] ADJECTIVE

In a state of ill temper or indigestion.

(**1737** G. O'FENAUGHTY *How to Converse with Children and the Exorbitantly Old*) **p 47** For instance, "Aw, poor boo-boo; are we mulligrubs today? A bit too hasty with our tasty snack?"

See also **bradypeptic**

myropolist

(maɪˈrapɒlɪst) [from Latin *myropōla*, Greek *μυροπωλης* (from *μυρον*, unguent, perfume + *πωλης*, a seller)] NOUN

One who sells perfumes.

(**1744** H. DESBOROUGH. *The Village, wherein a good many things happened, poorly documented but worthy of later note*) **p 201** So claim the philosophers: of all the senses, from the persistent optical illusions and allusions of sight to the relentless lunacy of touch, it is that of smell which links strongest of all to our tingling memory. And so the people recollect still the visit of the myropolist. She arrived with the garish and decrepit tottering of a peacock upon a broken claw—sloping amongst the shacks at the town's edge in a billow of extravagant sleeves, her left toes missing within a fisherman's black boot, rasping as if with a thistle tucked in her purplish bosom where most people lodge their spineless hearts. And she smelled of pure dread, with a reeking, nearly visible aura of sickly green encircling tangled hair and a strange agelessness of face. E'en from the sanctuary of latched shutters and kerchiefs packed beneath the door, the people could catch her inimitably awful scent: like an egg gone rotten and concealed in an armpit, like vomit, like a barnyard's hell, like the sweat of the dead. But this was the myropolist, a most uncommon guest, and so in spite of such poor advertisements all the villagers with their aprons and bushels of hay thought it not too decadent a luxury to purchase but a tiny vial of perfume. From a hundred inexplicable pockets the myropolist pulled tinctures of mahogany, oil-of-rose, extract-of-hemlock, ambergris and cuttlefish ink; and to each person an individual fragrance which seemed, they vowed, an essence quintessentially their own. Yet upon payment of gold or bartered milk, there came always a warning: *beware,* the woman croaked. Though the people knew not why she might say such a thing, they soon remembered it. For swiftly did those potions and perfumes became a menace and a thrill overpowering, as the village transfigured unto a miasma of memory. The odor of the dairymaid's permeable wrists suddenly evoked a childhood night spent throwing apples in a bonfire, while the carpenter's scalp smelled of one's first spoken word, and the huntresses bore the aroma of the fish-stricken floods a decade ago, and the blacksmith with his hands aglow conjured the image of one's mother fallen asleep. When finally the myropolist wobbled off to markets elsewhere, nobody could stay away from one another's throats, inhaling with desperate giggles and tears, for what was *now* had at once become a distillation of the past. Now, when the villagers speak of the myropolist, they tell us that though never did they learn her name, they find themselves at times longing for her return.

See also **halit**

naricorn

('nɛərikɔːn) [Latin *nāris*, nostril, + *cornū*, horn] NOUN

A horny and scrolled cover protecting the nostrils of certain birds.

(**1804** L. BREHAUT. *The Menace and the Merit of Apparent Mediocrity*) **p 241** 'Tis a property of the numinous to dwell within obscure things. Goblins have been known to curl comfortably in ill-used thimbles, while it is known that elixirs of plaster and lilacs confer upon the drinker a brief period of ambidextrous feet. One may on occasion ignite explosions through the contrary twist of a brass doorknob, while in times of great political upheaval 'tis possible to glimpse speaking skulls in the excretions of rotund pill-bugs. Most bedeviling of all are the powers of naricorn, powers which require specific and secret and squalling recitations, and for the sake of our safety must never be named.

See also **ætites, chirm, gelatia, kae, lygure, shiterow**

nemoral

('nɛm(ə)rəl) [classical Latin *nemorālis* belonging to a wood or forest, frequenting woodland, from *nemor-*, *nemus* wood (cognate with ancient Greek νρμος, wood), Gaulish *nemeton*, holy grove), Old Irish *nemed*, holy place + *-ālis*, suffix denoting 'of the kind of'] ADJECTIVE

Belonging to a grove.

(**1785** J. COPSEY. *On Cultivating one's own Virtues*) **p 432** Of the four ethical categories, as bequeathed us by the philosophers and the nymphs of antiquity: one may be moral (boring), immoral (more pleasurable, indeed, but mentally taxing), amoral (rather a bit too fashionable in these ballroom days), or nemoral. This final option allows one the benefits of an impoverished and yet colossal decadence, obscenely sprawling limbs, and a highly erotic interweaving of nerve, nervure, and wanton vines—these being but a grove's logical consequence: if growth, then connection. Though with quiet austerity nemorality sanctions no violence, it does excuse the theft of such trifles as broken light, seeping water, and the rich, fertile matter of the dead rotting generously within the dark of the forest floor. A nemoral compass permits gluttony, believing not in original sin (for apples are a delicacy, and bear their seeds in the shape of a star). In the flickering chapels of a grove, any and all weddings are sanctified by the tangle of blooms: oak to fern, willow to bear, hawthorn to wolf and doe to doe—a perpetual spring, a lovely fall.

See also **chiminage, dendrolatous, diatyposis, interlucation, nervure, porraceous, rampick**

nervure

(ˈnəːvj(ʊ)ə) [from French, *nervure*, the vein in a leaf (attested 1719), vein in an insect's wing (1764); in Middle French denoting a leather or sinew strap used to strengthen a shield (1380) or, a relief line decorating a fabric (1514), or, moulding in a relief (1542); from *nerf*, Anglo-Norman and Middle French sinew or tendon + *-ure*, suffix denoting action or process, or the result thereof] NOUN

1. *The vein in an insect's wing*, or, 2. *the vein of a leaf.*

(**1854** G. ROWAN-COTHCART. *Towards Poise amongst the Other*) **p 102** One desires always to know the correct word, for conversational precision is a virtue in swift decline; indeed, one knows the proper term could scarcely be veins or capillaries or much less ardent arteries. There exists all sorts of instances in which one might require such an exact name: *the nervures flickered with currents of electricity as seen ne'er before*, the poet exults, or *how with gifted stratagem did the insect craft those shining nervures of its wings as indistinguishable from those of the high cottonwood*, a useful phrase should one want to seem quite educated. Or, pursuing of triumph in a little spat, consider *trees haven't got blood, imbecile, they have nervures*. But then again one must bear in mind that perpetual peril of social awkwardness, should one coarsely misuse this word in casual exchange. One must take care not to disparage the nervure or render it bawdy—*he is a weak as a nervure*, some scoff, or jeer at somebody gallivanting about town in *pantaloons so lacy-thin they might as well be nervures*. Aye, remember that there do exist those people who must forever guard against the

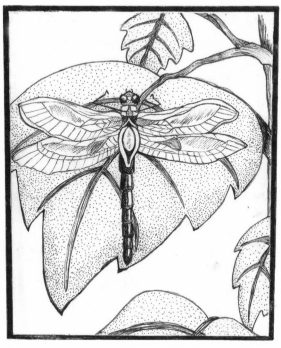

minute fury of a paper cut, and wear hunched overcoats in concealment of certain aerial capacities, who even in times of romance must never trip in their ice skates; these far-flung members of our blurring species possess not an aorta but a system of nervures, and bleed in pulsing chlorophyll, and others conceal the personal elation of a tight-folded and spectacular, transluculent wing—and, naturally, desire not to reveal their private frailty and perilous power to the mocking envy of the mammalian public at large.

See also **chiminage, dendrolatous, diatyposis, holophanerosis, interlucation, nemoral, porraceous, rampick**

noyade

(nwaːˌjad) [French *noyade* (1794), from *noyer*, to kill by drowning; from post-classical Latin *necare*, to kill by drowning, a specialized use of classical Latin **necāre**, to kill] NOUN

Execution by drowning.

(**1872** F. KELLARD. *A Lengthy History of Art's Great Secrets, with images as Proof*) **p 139** The jubilant Eros, with his plump nudity and his trumpet of transgression, was to be executed by drowning. So 'twas decreed by all those citizens who dwell in silent immobility within our paintings: by the icon of blue Philosopher with his robes fading into the temple of tempera, and unanimously agreed by the well-proportioned rabbit, the plaster Venus with her garlands of pansies and dangerous spring, even by the aureate haystack beneath a landscape's excessively fluid and unchanging sky. For death by watercolor has always been the preferred method of capital punishment within the society of art. Had the little cherub not committed that greatest crime, perhaps the sentence might not have been so harsh, but alas, 'twas true: the Eros had made music—a noise so audibly *real*. His horn had resounded with a tremulous tone that echoed from frame to fool's-gold frame and deafened the unsuspecting satyr, scandalizing the innocent drawing of a tousled terrier. And a sound generated in a picture shall never be forgiven. The condemned was kept imprisoned within a still-life, where every pear and mouse skull was a *memento mori*, and was guarded by a saint periodically stricken by visions of the hells above our heads. The judge was to be the duchess, her portrait flawless down to each mole and her half-hidden pregnancy; in wait of the spectacle, a great parade of peasants bearing morbid bread danced wild in the oily square. The mannerist cats remained apathetic, and aesthetically plump. Convicted, breathless, and doomed, Eros displayed nonetheless a calm perhaps fundamental to a resident of a fresco who from the domed ceiling peers down upon so many people kneeling in ecstasy upon the stones. Watercolor, he explained with a martyr's tranquility to all the illustrated world, was not a thing he feared, for when the noyade engulfed him he understood that in its dissipating image his being would be not lifeless, but transformed.

See also **rhyparography**

nubivagant

('njuːbɪvəˌgænt)   [Latin *nūbivagus*, wandering among the clouds (from *nūbēs*, cloud) + *vag-*, denoting movement (from *vagērī*, to roam) + *-ant*, suffix designating adjective function]
ADJECTIVE

Passing through clouds.

(**1767**   L. B. GESTENYA.   *Reports from a place not-so-far*)
p 901   I see it now, aye, and scarcely can I see. Here in the nubivagant realm, the external world is defined only by the degree to which it is obscured. I should like to describe this place as fraught with fog like violence in that moment before it occurs, or like an incessant somnolence over a complicated, bountiful world, but of this I cannot be sure. Before I came to this place, I believe that others could recognize my face, and recollect my name. But here amidst the clouds, that-which-exists is contingent upon the possibility of mystery; that is, all things take on their being in accordance with their concealment; that is, the reality of objects, of spires, of panicked bats and twig and the spectral moon, lies only in their ability to be lost in the slithering mists. In this case, I myself am among the most real entities in this world.

See also **i-what, ughten, versipellous, vespertilionize**

nucha

('nju:kə) [post-classical Latin *nucha*, spinal cord (cited 11th century in the works of Arabic-Latin translator Constantine Africanus; from circa 1200 in British sources), nape of the neck (from late 12th century in British sources); ultimately from Arabic physicians' *nukā*, spinal marrow, later confused with *nuqra*, nape of the neck] NOUN

1. *The nape of one's neck*, or, 2. *the spinal cord.*

(**1891** ROSEBLADE & GILFEATHER. *A Diary of Love among the Early Dead, and Childhood Lost*) **p 162** This was the first part of you which I began to love. For having lost the invisibility of innocence, and innocence's own unreality, our two bodies grew so dense I could not sleep for all the solidity of hip; so shy was I as to believe that to utter the lick of your name would rupture my tongue. But I could watch your nucha with impunity, creeping behind you with the hushed step which I had learned from the midnight shrews. And so unexpectedly did your neck possess its own secret perfection, and I knew I was likely the only one to notice—this transfixion, this trail of downy hair, and that sweetness of spine in all its infinitely breakable anguish.

See also **frantling, homœoteleuton, quicquidlibet, supernatant, ycore**

nyctograph

('nɪktə(ʊ)grɑːf) [from Greek *nycto-*, *νυκτο*, night + *-graph*, from Latin *graphos*, Greek *γραφος*, written, or a writer. See French *nyctographe*, machine enabling the blind to write or the sighted to write in the dark (invented 1818-19 or earlier), and Hellenistic Greek *noctographia*, *νυκτογραφία*, writing by night. Word *nyctograph* and a corresponding device invented by mathematician and writer Charles Dodgson (Lewis Carroll)] NOUN

A device for recording one's ideas when half awake or at night.

(1831 ANONYMOUS, & M. ENDELDOW, ED. *Sundry letters unearthed in the early hours*) **p 49** Item CVII, found in the Children's Cloisters of Blessed Anglia: I will not remember this when I wake up, I know I will not—when the morning comes it will come as they say the archangels will, falling on our chests with resplendent powers of asphyxiation. But the archangels never arrive, and the morning always does; tomorrow I will wake inhaling sunlight, and when I rise from the rumpled country of my bed I won't remember what I am writing or how I wrote it, should fate or the superior eyes permit me even to glimpse it one more time. I know I will not. I shall conceal it before I fall to sleep again, in silence and shame taking care not to rouse the other children—for here, we are all a tapestry of interwoven fingers against the eyes, or we are traitors with mouths open in hunger, betrayal, apology. I will not remember where it lies. Already I feel myself slipping back into unmapped sleep—warped caverns and glades of damp complexity into which no hawk's eyes can see, sleep here is a topography of escape—I write this swiftly, forgetting words because in sleep we carry some things with us, and other things we may finally abandon in our momentary flight. I must, must write of my dream, even though we are told that visions are meaningless and probably a sin. But I dreamt of outside, outside the cloisters. There, all things were different because Moral Lessons did not exist, and neither did soap which scrapes the skin, and neither did our benevolent guardians or locked doors. In the outside all the children were brave and attended by armies of robins with bloody breasts. And we carried not spoons and bowls but flutes and swords, and this was us and there was no one else. But my brow aches already from kneeling upon the very clean floor, anticipating the bells which will scream their own clamorous names, there in the steeple which each morn sees us all and knows what we are. I must hide this, hide it now, and in the morning I will not remember where I hid it or even how I wrote it or even that this moment happened or even that I had a wonderful unholy dream— but I did write this and it did happen and I did dream and I did hide it and they cannot make that disappear.

See also **ughten**

ombrifuge

(ˈɒmbrɨfjuːdʒ) [from Greek *ombros*, ὄμβρος, + *-fuge*, from Latin *fugĕre*, to flee] NOUN

A shelter against the rain, chiefly, an umbrella.

(**1818** P. NISBITT. *A Useful Apparatus*) **p 18** The human romance with the umbrella equates to a long lineage of tremendous creativity, since its invention in Mesopotamia, when cuneiform philosophies were written in mud, and its adoption in ancient Egypt, in which entire trains of subservient priests dedicated their lives to following immortal cats with shades against the asps' bite of the sun. In India's past, monarchs bore their umbrellas on the backs of elephants whose perfume congealed to form soft bells, and in China it was painted umbrellas which permitted the ascent of certain insubstantial poets into the mists of autumn peaks. Please note, then, the fact that the underside of a well-used ombrifuge, so soaked in decades of sun and doleful storm, tends to eventually develop within it a miniature and private sky.

See also **isokeraunic**

opsony

(ɒpˈsɒniː) [Latin *opsōnium*, provisions for a meal, victuals, or Hellenistic Greek *opsonion*, ὄψώνιον, provisions, usually wages or pay towards the purchase of *opson*, ὄψον, cooked food, relish, rich fare, delicacies, of unknown origin + *onios*, ὤνιος, for sale] NOUN

Anything which is eaten with or spread upon bread.

(**1804** CALDERWOOD & BUNTON. *The Dubious Cookery: A Culinary Catalogue*) **p 180** Mustard; pesto; layers of sparkling dust (containing possible gold); pickles; ketchup of far China; approximately one thousand and seven hundred species of cheese (including those of dubious palatability curdled from the milk of the domestic cat); marinara (delicious with basil); mayonnaise; jam (different from jelly, with its ghoulish art of the jiggle); honey (which shall be your favorite, sweetly pollinating your belief in altruism); alfredo sauce; plaster-of-Paris; rainwater; heavenly elixirs which in excess may cause gout; butter with parsley; pulped artichokes or Olympian olives or ethereal salt; powdered arithmetic (we shall leave you to comprehend this sourest opsony in your own lonesome and ravenous nights); cinnamon and sugar (mixed).

See also **pantler**

oudemian

('əʊdiːmiːən) [Greek *oudemia*, οὐδεμία, from *oudeis*, οὐδείς, no, none, not (of uncertain origin within the Greek language) + -*de* (also of uncertain origin) + μία, one + -*an*, suffix denoting type] ADJECTIVE

Nonexistent, unreal; employed in the literary nonsense-phrase "Oudemian Street"(1593) to designate the notional address of nowhere.

(1709(?)-1907(?)) BYRD & ASHE. *On the Prospects of Didacticism under a New Moon*) **p I** Were we to give the academy a definite name, we might call it the Oudemian School—of course, we are not certain we have so christened it. Nor may we invite your visitation, inasmuch as we can say not precisely where it is: perhaps on a dirt lane of unopened bougainvillea in multifarious, shifting shades, or at other times (maybe), it sits upon the meadows at the bottom of the sea, or at the latitude and longitude of absolute zero upon the unobserved moon. There is a chimney but no hearth; within the corridors, admittedly, a compass upheld whirls a sarabande and pinpoints the fidelity of no magnetic pole, though there are indeed aurora. No curriculum repeats itself, though non-Euclidean geometry is put into active practice and negative numbers are regularly multiplied to equate to a positive candlestick. Courses of history trace a chronology of hoaxes, and in the studios we possess gilded frames but lack the angelic paintings to fill them, and horticulture focuses upon the finest manner in which to dig a hole. We believe we possess a fine library of books lacking indices, magnificent tales lacking end, and a dictionary referencing sources entirely unwritten and subsequently defining no word beyond the space between its calligraphic characters. Moreover (and this does not represent a problem), the students remain perpetually absent, without excuse. *Cogito, ergo sum*—or so it is said—but so have we refuted the philosopher, existing precisely because we do not think.

See also **anachorism, byss, i-hwat, nubivagant, ughten, umbration, versipellous, vorago**

pandiculation

(pandɪkjʊ'leɪʃ(ə)n) [French *pandiculation* (1587) in Middle French; also as *pendiculation* ; Latin *pandiculāt-*, past participial stem of *pandiculārī* + French *–ion*, suffix denoting condition or action] NOUN

The act of stretching as a result of sleepiness, or yawning.

(**1820**, L. L. LUX. *Mme. Lilith's Guide to Laws of Etiquette, and of Being Interesting in a Parlour*) **p 80** One must try to practice one's pandiculation daily, as it is reported in the *Journal of Antemeridian Medicine* that studies reveal it to be crucial in establishing the proper flow of blood to the feet. The true art of pandiculation, however, has been cultivated to a spiritual practice and mastered by the domestic housecats, *Felis catus*, who still refuse to divulge their secrets.

See also **ailurophile, tibert, ycore**

pantler

(ˈpantlə(r)) [Probably a variant of *panter,* Anglo-Norman *paneter, panetier, pannetier, paintier, a* pantry-man, baker (Old French *panetier*), perhaps a variant of *butler,* an office with which the pantler later merged. No equivalent form of *pantler* exists in Latin, although compare with *pantleria,* pantry] NOUN

Officer in a household in charge of bread.

(**1738** H. TREFFRY. *Those professions most delicious, and likely to behoove the Young Citizen in Search of Decency and meals*) **p 254** Pantlerism: a most excellent career choice. Let us begin our vocational training immediately, with jam.

See also **opsony**

papyriferous

(ˌpapɨˈrɪf(ə)rəs) [Latin *papȳrifer,* papyrus-bearing (from *papȳrus,* a manuscript written upon fibres of the papyrus plant *Cyperus papyrus*) + *-ferous,* suffix with unlimited number of derivatives denoting production or creation] ADJECTIVE

Producing paper, papyrus, or items thereof.

(**1901** THIRD COMMITTEE IN THE INTERESTS OF CONVENIENCE, ET AL. *A Tirade Against the Unions, for the bewildered bourgeoisie*) **p 23** Heartlessly must we hope that the child laborers of the papyriferous factories do not grow weary of their working conditions, the unavoidable and gruesome paper cuts and the pulp lodged in the struggling lung, for should they form a guild and realize the potential of organized protest, we shall find ourselves stupefied in a great famine of folded things: no cranes, no paper jackdaws with their rustling cry of *kae, kae, kae,* no eerily gliding balloons, no crinkled flowers which continuously unfurl themselves in triangles, no creased toads to double as love notes. Desperate, we would struggle to hold out against the rebellion of the workforce, but no doubt our longing for the world of paper would soon force us to crumple.

See also **kae**

phasma

(ˈfazmə) [Latin *phasma*, spectre, apparition (later adopted as genus name), Greek *phasma*, φάσμα, spectre, apparition, phantom (from *phainô*, φάίνειν, to show or appear)] NOUN

I. *The appearance of anything fantastic, such as a meteor, or,* 2. *an apparition or phantom, or,* 3. *a "walking stick" insect of the genus* Phasmitidae, *known for their ability to mimic twigs; these insects may possess spines or a terrible smell, and in large numbers may devastate oak trees.*

(1851   E. GALLIEN.   *True Declarations of an eminent Astronomer: A Defensive Treatise*) **p 289**   While I recognize that my colleagues—indeed, all you scientists whose beards are tangled with crumbs and nebulae, you critics with your unimaginative fangs—may name my theory as mere madness, and call my discovery not a profound revelation but only the addlepated illogical leap of an old astronomer fallen into a drooling nap in his observatory. Over decades of dedication and the sudden warping of the world unto non-Euclidean geometry, oft have I been discredited (though still I maintain that it was *I* who first detected Neptune and its oceanic pull). But now shall I be redeemed, for I have determined the true nature of the meteor. Of course even farmboys and tigers have born witness to those showers of sparks causing a stellar panic in December or the summer's dog days, and some have gone so far as to speculate that those weird and weighty stones found sprayed across terrestrial sands are but meteoric diamonds, stones briefly given the form of a star.

But no! it is I who in my own garden where the moon skims the open tulips and casts pollen over my hoary hair, I who have glimpsed, and heard and even held the meteors. No stones are they, but frail and devious beings grinding their mandibles amidst the acorns, little lives of devious legs, tiny animate phenomena who have crawled up my sleeves and across my butterfly clavicles. A meteor, I have found, has the baffling appearance of a twig. I loved them, I did. And say not that I am mad! I shall present my empirical observations at the coming meeting of the Queen's Society of the Skies, to which I am certain I shall be invited, whereupon all shall understand this lush and terribly vast, awfully brilliant universe to be far more interwoven with our open hands than once we had believed. I shall admit I have lost my meteor, as with the subtlety of all cosmic things it has shivered and slipped away, though assiduously I search the wise and wizened oak grove for my fallen stars; I miss them.

See also **balanoid, catabibazon, quercivorous, selenite, selentic**

pheal

('fïːəl) [Imitative, onomatopoeic] NOUN

The cry of a hunting jackal.

(**1867** H. J. CLOTHOS. *Somnolence and Fear*) **p 349** *Help me now*, the Lady Eugenia did plead, with a voice trembling and thin, high as a flute in wind across the tarnished equatorial sky. Such is the tone a noble takes solely in true fear, and so I listened. I, the shrouded soothsayer, I the woman of oracular sight and common blood, I the thorny old one in my alleyway hole, I, the teller of fates to whom only the ague-stricken poor and the superstitious travelers do come—until that grey eve, when the Lady Eugenia descended in a storm of white skirts from her palace of chandeliers and dovecotes far above the city's cold lanes. She came to beg visions of me. *I hear it*, whispered she, *and never am I free*. She beseeched me to listen and to hear it too: that scream, the yelp of the lapdog's frenzied dream, she said, the howl of hunger tinted with red and deadly as the sirens. *Never have I glimpsed the jackal*, she told me, *but I hear it still*. I heard not her pheal, but this I did not say. In the sort of pity which never before had I nursed for one of high descent—and yet a woman of mercy am I—I searched the tarot cards with their mocking signs of the moon, and so I saw; in the Lady's silken palms I read lines of life and the bifurcating heart, and so I saw; in one of the dire agonies which is my gift of the fortune teller's miraculous trance, and so I saw. *It asks of where I am*, said Eugenia; she shrank in discuss from my missing fingertips

174

and from the wings of the dead pigeons lying upon the dirty floor, and she was afraid. I saw. *I confess*, the Lady told me, *that at night I come near to heeding its call. There it is*, and her gasp was the beginning of her vanishing. *Can not you hear it too? What can the pheal possibly mean?* But I, I the seer of the streets and I the eater of bones, I am a woman of mercy, and so I did not reply.

See also **catacoustics**

porphyrogenite

(ˌpɔ fɨˈrɒdʒɨnʌɪt) [Latin *porphyrogenitus*, Byzantine Greek πορφυρογέννητος, from ancient *porphyro*, ΠΟΡΦΥΡΟ, purple + γέννητός, birthing] NOUN, or, ADJECTIVE

1. *A member of the imperial family of the Byzantine Empire at Constantinople (330-1453 C.E.), whose legitimacy as heir to throne was reputedly conferred by a birth in a purple-hung chamber, tinted with a violet dye of the mineral porphyry,* or, 2. *purple of this color.*

(1751 N. GOODFELLOW. *The Aesthetic Improbable*) p 109 The dynasty has long since dwindled into an adulteration of adultery, bastardry, and infants lost, and the kingdom collapsed into a labyrinth beneath the earth. Yet still can one recognize the last revenants of the royal family— the decaying porphyrogenites—now kneeling before we commoners ourselves. It is that certain shade within the skin of the pauper shambling between brothel and barrel of rotting fish, a hue like twilight fossilized, like the seashell embedded in a veiled wall. It is the decayed dignity still lending a dusky shade to the tramp's frayed cloak, and the child birthed in secret and straightaway abandoned to the alley dogs, its face a deep porphyrogenite split by the very first scream. It is the livid hands of the penniless madman gesticulating to an absent court from the gutter with its lustrous scum, preaching maniacal purple prose; we pass the grime-headed heirs to the empire and avoid meeting their mismatched eyes, though in tribute we shall occasionally toss a coin.

See also **coquelicot, watchet, xanthopsia**

porraceous

(pəˈreɪʃəs) [Latin *porrāceus*, resembling a leek, leek-green (*porrum*, leek + - *āceus*, suffix denoting 'of the nature of')] NOUN, or, ADJECTIVE

Green, comparable to a leek.

(**1751** N. GOODFELLOW. *The Aesthetic Improbable*) **p 100** Much time has passed, as does drool from the mouths of senile wizards, since the great vegetarian movement among the poets. Now so many scribes will ravenously stuff boars' heads with apples or thrushes and with bare teeth tear out the throats of raw pheasants, but for a now-romanticized time all verse was dictated by the herbivores' pentameter. Still one may sift through such superlative, influential volumes as *Thoughts upon an autumn radish* or *Leaves of Salad*, or enjoy the shocking biographies of bards who willingly permitted grapevines to gnaw away at their flesh over inebriated decades, who made moaning love to harems of celery. Indeed, no true literary connoisseur can possibly refrain from an eye welling with opaque tears upon the recitation of *Ode to the Onion's Heart*, or such lines as *how adoration lurks, voracious, for all thy glow, my beloved most porraceous.* O, to the glory of the Leek!

See also **coquelicot, dendrolatrous, diatyposis, nemoral, nervure**

pyrame

(paɪreɪm) [Latin *pȳrāmus*, from Greek *pyramis*, πυραμίς, pyramid] NOUN

A term employed by John of Trevisa, in his 1398 translation of the proto-encyclopedia of Bartolomeus, De Proprietatibus Rerum, *applied to the cones, rays, or pencils of light which enter the human eye as communicated by objects.*

(**1649** L. FELHAM. *The Senses, as explained in terms applying to Nobles and to cats*) So it be decreed that should we know this world we shalt be permitted ne'er amputation, but must ever be linked to all other things, through lines as thin and imperceptible as phantasms' veins, a geometry not solely of vision, but of touch and scream, voice and speaking silence, perfume and tongue and the feel of ink upon hand. We are our pyrames; we exist in fascination.

See also **gelatia**, **uloid**

pyrausta

(paɪraʊstə) [Latin *pyrausta* (from the naturalist Pliny, although the reading is disputed; given as equivalent to *pyrallis*, denoting either a fiery insect or a pigeon), from ancient Greek *pyraustês*, πυραύστης, a moth that gets singed in a candle, πῦρ (see *pyro*, fire), + αὔειν to ignite. The classical Latin word was later adopted into taxonomy as *Pyrausta*, name of a genus of moths] NOUN

A fabulous insect supposed to live in fire, which will die if taken from it.

(**1533**   ANONYMOUS. *Bestiarium Maestitia*) **p 14**   We find them scatter'd round our bonfires, when the Solstice hath come to its close and the Cinders hath fallen as so shall we all. 'Round our dead torches are the Little Corpses array'd, and when we do douse our Candles a Brief Bodie shall flutter in a sorrow'd Spirale from the Smoke. For the Pyrausta can liveth not without the Fire 'pon which it Feeds, with its Tongue of Wick and Panick, and so shall we murder't each time we blowen the light away. So be we all Butchers. But Birthers be we, too, for we æternally desire to keep ourselves in Light, and escape the Night's Dominion. Never will we abandon our belov'd flames. We shall never cease to illumine the World, and so shall the Pyraustas be fore'er Brungen into Being, for we be afear'd of the Dark.

See also **amphisbaena**, **barghest**, **bucentaur**, **dipsas**, **mamuque**,
scytale, **urisk**, **wasserman**, **yale**

qualtagh

('kwɑ:ltəx) [From Manx *quaaltagh*, literally 'someone who meets or is met,' from *quaail*, meeting, also action of meeting + *-agh*, suffix forming adjectives and also nouns expressing belonging. Insertion of *-t-* perhaps an association with Old Irish *comaltae*, foster-brother, companion; see Scottish Gaelic *còmhdhalaiche*, someone who meets or is met, *deagh-chòmhalaiche*, someone whom one is lucky to meet, *droch-chòmhalaiche*, someone who is unlucky to meet.] NOUN

The first person one encounters after leaving the home upon a special day, such as the New Year.

(**1887** G. HORNBEAM. *The Comedies of Being Special*) **p 118** The morning following the final masquerade ball of a decadent December, when all was a bedlam of satin and vomit and feathers strewn like wealth across the floor, Elmo awoke with a groan among the other unconscious dancers; the voided eyes of the masks watched him in haughty ghoulishness, as he slumped out of the courtyard and into the too-rutted street. In the barnyard, Elvira heaved aside her blankets of hay and trudged into town to purchase a loaf of bread soft enough to gum between two remaining teeth. Emeric donned his cap and his secretly magic spectacles, beginning the daily walk to the library's leonine doors. Securitizing the early enigma of the sky through painted lash, Enid decided the rains ought not to fall today, not with any moral justification, and departed upon slippers of stolen silk. With all the logical irrationality belonging to a scamp three years of age,

Erasmus rubbed his eyes and chased a refugee chicken over the cobblestones, and down the lane and over the shoe-sanctified bridge. Crawling from the scullery bed, Elspeth followed a slight shade humming at the corner of her vision, a ghost wavering its way from window to prismatic window to peer inside with invisible and prurient eyes. But this was the year's beribboned birth, and so Emeric collided with the still-inebriated Elmo, unintentionally letting loose an eloquent and literary curse, and turning a corner elegant Enid knocked the tender lung of the bread from Elvira's bony arms. And finding that warm exhalation of yeast, Erasmus cupped his hands, spicing it with peppery filth as he cupped his hands in mute offering to Elspeth, haunted by shadows and soot. Thus was January delivered, as tragic newborns on occasion arrive with the morning mail, and a dozen eyes ignored the dawn to gaze at one another's at once mesmerizing moles. And each was for a moment the most important person in the world, for the laws of probability do dictate that each of us will inevitably be somebody's qualtagh, at some point in our precious lives.

See also **fernticle**, **umbration**, **yepsen**

quandros*

('kwandrəʊs) [From John Trevisa's translation of Bartolo-
maeus' 1398 *De Proprietatibus Rerum* (*On the Properties of Things*),
Book XVI:84, "*quadros* is a stone of vile coulour, but it is of
great virtue, as Diosc. saith, and is found in the head of a vulture, and helpeth against all evill causes, and filleth teates full of
milke," and see also Sir Thomas Browne's 1684 *Musæum Clausum*
III:7, "A noble *Quandros*, or stone taken out of a vulture's head."]
NOUN

*A stone supposedly possessing magical powers, taken from a vulture's
skull.*

(**1685** E. ELLYLL. *De Penna*) **p 13** I have been the
warrior, hewn by a sword whose hilt bears the likeness of
a unicorn, *argent sinistre*, the battlefield's stricken ornament;
and I have been the beggar, collapsed amid the rusted
barrows and bones of the roadside with two coins for his
eyes clenched in one hand. The fawn I have been, dappled
innocence, fallen in the meadow of poppies and somnolent
bees with ribs exposed. I have been carrion. But I have
been too the vulture, gorgeously hideous, wizened as a sage
and bald as an oracular crone, my beak all hooked cruelty.
I have known the necessary pleasure of tearing flesh, and
the extraordinary taste of decay—indescribable, save as an
evocation perhaps of certain temptations we have loved,
the shadow side of milk and honey. Flight have I known,
the sheer marvel of the animal aloft and the body one more
element of wind, and as the vulture I have died. I have
been the quandros, the stone whose hue is that of mingled

blood and mud, whose texture is too intimate, a treasure held in the mortal hand as a memoriam of throbbing, wheeling, relentless life.

> ° NOTE This word, while remaining adamantly existent in the history of letters, humming its elegies and runes within the echoing texts of Trevisa and Browne, does not appear within the *Oxford English Dictionary*. It is omitted, or forgotten, consigned now to a sort of rich oblivion. One may perhaps consider it thus a false word, or one too particular, too scarce, too much a cadaver to enter the lexicon. And yet, as the author would posit, it is this very rarity and amnesia and meaninglessness, which renders *quandros* a perfect member of the language, a subtle and hollow and absent being like any other word.

quercivorous

(kwɜːˈsɪvərəs) [Latin *querci-*, combining form of *quercus*, oak + *vorous*, devouring, eating]

Feeding upon the leaves of oaks.

(**1682** REV. N. M. ANSTICE. *On the Proper Penalties of Witches: a historie*) **p 47** And so did Eva flee, having feasted upon the glossy leaf of the Splendid Oak, most primordial of beings within the parish so bless'd that the very dusk paused that it might lengthen the wails of the evening prayer. Had only fool Eva prepared a salad from the Chestnut, or infused the buds of the humble Elm into a Fascinating Tea, mayhap her offense should not have been one of such severity, but a small Sin warranting only a day in the stocks. But she did stand at the cemetery's edge, as the rainfall reprimanded her skin and the Oak groaned low, and she did eat with joyful gluttony those manifold leaves. And a Quercivorous Crime shall ne'er be forgiven. When the Sheriffs issued the Writ of Prosecution, calling for her immediate arrest and a clatter of shackles 'round her fleet and filthy ankles, a host of villagers bearing torches and the stench of frankincense spread to knock upon doors, to overturn barrels of pickled fish, to threaten the traitorous wind. But already Eva had vanished without print-of-foot and without apology, as do hide the faeries and the minxes in winter. And with what cunning didst she conceal herself in the most unexpected place, where none might search: for Eva did curl within the hollow heart of the Oak itself, the tree having been complicit in the entire affair.

See also **latitant, phasma**

quicquidlibet

(ˈkwɪkwɪdlɪbɛt) [from Latin *quicquid libet, from quicquid, quidquid,* whatever (reduplication of *quid,* anything) + *libet,* it pleases; expansion of classical *quodlibet,* a fantasia or a philosophical question] NOUN

Whatever one pleases, anything whatsoever.

(**1899** S. E. ENDYMION. *Ambiguous Sounds, or, nimble words, or, manners of speaking to one's Sweetheart*) **p 301** The lover arrives; his wrists are translucent, transforming, revealing the hieroglyphs and heat of veins coursing beneath. The lover turns, and the nape of her neck— the nucha inimitable, inestimable, aglow—is a flowerbed of unseen bones. *Quicquidlibet,* you say, and the lover may not understand. But incomprehension makes the word whatever one desires it to be, and from your own vivisection and the lover's gasp comes the secret meaning, a humming thread wending its way out of us and over our bent heads and amplifying and magnifying and reinventing all, until we exist wholly within the infinitely possible world of all we are willing to give and to take.

See also **bucentaur, fremitus, i-hwat, nucha, ycore**

rampick

('ræmpɪk) [Of obscure origin, possibly from *pike*, a point or a spike, apparent throughout a complex borrowing of Romance and Germanic languages] NOUN

A tree possessing a decayed or dead crown.

(**1763** REDGEWELL & CREAK. *What happened in the forest*) **p 209** The woods were haunted, and irreparably so: the ghosts visited the villagers each horrifyingly winsome night, most severely upon those evenings when the moon took on its more fluid properties. The people could hear the scrabbles and scratches of clawed twigs against warped windowpanes, the creak of unearthed roots just beyond the futilely charmed doors. *Come out. . .* called the rustles, called the cracks and the snaps. 'Twas the rampicks, demanding regeneration, regrowth, and revenge; the rotting ghouls of the headless trees had now come back from the mulch.

See also **chiminage, dendrolatous, diatyposis, interlucation, nemoral, nervure, porraceous**

rheotaxis

(riːəʊˌtæksɪs) [adapted from Greek *rheo*, ῥέος, stream or current, and *taxis*, τάξις, arrangement, order] NOUN

The movement of an organism in response to running water.

(**1894** H. PEAGRAM. *A Marriage of True Binds*) **p 34**
Edna and Elbert ought to have recognized the arrival far earlier than they did. Of course, one can claim not that the pair neglected to notice the signs, but rather chose to ignore them, as one ignores a superior's burp. Pipes shall forever make a certain amount of noise, after all, particularly when the extravagance of indoor plumbing proves too avant-garde for a crone and a wizardly old man. But Edna had insisted upon this decidedly pricey matter: that highly necessary switch to the faucet's miracle nose. Still, when Edna and Elbert heard that additional chatter among the typical whine of hot water pumping through their house, they perhaps should have expected what came next. But it is said that sound carries best through a liquid, not out of it, not up into our insubstantial world. So that clacking and the cryptic din was clearest when the two pressed wrinkled ears against the generous despot of the boiler in their closet. According to Edna, the noise sounded like nothing so much as somebody repeating *thee blow laxity*, over and over again in dire absurdity, which Elbert found to be a highly imbecilic thought. Indeed, already Elbert had his suspicions, which he did not disclose. And he had the nerve to feign ignorance when she demanded whether he might know the cause behind their habitually clogged

drains, the weeds boiling from the gutters as an unholy green host. He merely shrugged, toddling away to pick more apricots with which to overfeed the rather corpulent mule. After the mysterious congestion of their toilet and its overflow into the garden, Edna's daisies withered with an audible cough and died in concert, and the wild doves altered the ballets of their pale flights in order to avoid the stinking aura over the roof. Though well aware that soon enough things would reach their inevitable close, Elbert kept his hush. It was, of course, a rainy day when finally the culmination came, when Edna took a bath in order to ease her aching bones with lye. She was scrubbing the webs of her toes, half-hidden by pearlescent bubbles and incandescent dirt, when she let out the shriek. From the slowly flooding kitchen Elbert snorted into his teacup, knowing with delicious satisfaction that the baby turtles, clicking and droning their joyous rheotaxis, had at last erupted into the tub.

See also **motatorious**

rhyparography

(rɪpəˈrɒgrəfɪ) [from late Latin *rhyparographos,* = Greek *rhupara-graphos,* ῥυπαρογράφος, from *rhuparos,* ῥυπαρός filthy] NOUN

The painting of mean or distasteful subjects.

(**1782** COMMITTEE FOR REFORM OF ART &
MOST OBJECTS, ET AL. *A Tract Against the Augmentation of
Corruption in Our Times*) **p 20** None may deny it: the work
is simply disgusting. Not for nothing do these hordes
of clergy and aestheticians besiege the musæum, roping
themselves to the decorous columns and crying pleas to
the sculpture of bleak Justice with her eyes eroded and
blank. The subject matter is not only prurient but far too
lowly to merit portrayal even by a shadow, let alone this
brazen display. Moreover, the style is not something we
appreciate: as we have experienced it, nudity does not in
any manner resemble some happy piano, nor are thighs
such a hybrid of crystal and red, nor are they so flexible;
we do hope the moon would never do something so sordid
as that. And the slug is simply unnecessary. We dislike
the manner in which the cat-hairs of the artist's brush
have become embedded in the pigment, which smells still
of flesh. One can only imagine the perverse painter who
would perpetrate such a foul deviation of many-jointed
legs, this image hovering in the clouds of incense between
pornography and poor poem. We plan on removing the
rhyparography and consigning it to the tongues not of
sensuality but of flames, but at the moment we are having
difficulty looking away.

See also **frazil, hederated, limax, noyade**

rifacimento

(rifatʃi›mento) [adopted Italian *rifacimento*, from *rifac-*, stem of *rifare*, to remake.] NOUN

A new-modeling or recasting of a literary work.

(**1800** PUMPHREY & COOTES. *Essays Upon Literature, and its influences possibly Corruptive or otherwise Odd*) **p 312** Upon its composition in 1395, inscribed by the thorned hands of blind and famished monks upon a desolate isle in the Irish sea, the *Biblio Dolos* was considered to be a flawless manifesto of the Goodness to which must we all aspire. For did not the illuminated lynx upon the letter *E* bow its tail with such humility, such grace, in the grinning face of the Black Death? When the printing press was birthed in a great bloodletting of typeface and sharp serifs, the work was distributed with much success, but seemed somewhat altered: the lynx had crept to an unknown page, and new words which had not been known to exist sidled their unpronounceable way betwixt the psalms. If tapped, the spines of the book released a scent similar to that of the indigo sweet pea, but soon invited the hordes of barbarian bookworms, whose tunnels regrettably obliterated a number of quite pious phrases with the addition of fresh storylines, convoluted and dark. By 1520, the book seemed not at all what it had been before, rather a tumultuous adventure involving corsairs and scullery maids in disguise, and certain motifs appeared a bit too often for the reader's comfort. The papacy condemned any lithe interpretations of the seventh chapter, to no avail. In the fifth edition, circa 1581, the *Biblio Dolos* seemed not prose but an epical poem of irregular rhymes and ambitiously modern punctuation; in 1618 it became apparent that now Europe held in its hands not a proper book at all but an audacious play, comedic in tone and cataclysmic in climax, in which an overpopulation of spurious characters entered and exited and switched genders far too often for the costumers to manage beneath plumed hats and cosmetic kohl. The heretics suggested that in fact all we nobles and sages and serfs had in truth whiled away hundreds of years of galleons and plagues in reciting this very drama, performing unawares in the courts and the taverns, and though censured with each rifacimento the idea began to take the weight of a migraine within our scandalized minds. We hear salivating verses, rapidly decaying and revivified lines whispered in the streets while a bright bobtail passes behind a cornerstone, and whirl around to find only the nothingness, and in this the dawn or perhaps the twilight of a century, we cannot know what shall become of the book—what will happen?

See also **chorizont, homœoteleuton, scytale**

scytale

('sɪtəli:) [adopted Latin *scytalē*, Greek *skutalê*, σκυτάλη, staff]
NOUN

I. *A serpent mentioned by ancient writers, resembling a cylindrical staff of uniform thickness, or,* 2. *A method of secret writing, practiced in Sparta, in which a strip of writing was wound around a tapering staff so that the writing could not be read, and could only be interpreted when wound around a staff of precisely the right form and size.*

(**1533** ANONYMOUS. *Bestiarium Maestitia*) **p 17** There be but a lone Scytale left upon this Earthe, though in poesie do we find much telling of its Being. *The serpente, sayeth the Poet, shineth with such a diuersitie of speckles upon his backe that all that look thereon haue wonder.* Aye, once did they crawl the Wastes where none might roam save the paws of that Dog-star agleam, and spake ne'er to Journeyman nor parch'd Sage. 'Twas the task of the aging warrior to wind the Serpente 'round its proper stave, mayhap to tell that True Story of the Lightning that is our Life, and sure the other would lead the soldier to Jackals and the Abyss. Now be the Scytales lost, but for One who lieth hidden in the dust. We seek its secretes, though we believe there be but one stick that might reveal to us the Wyrds. We be much afear'd, for should we wind the Serpente 'round a crook'd staff, what erroneous Tale shall rear its head, and swallow us all?

See also **amphisbaena, barghest, bucentaur, dipsas, homœoteleuton, mamuque, pyrausta, rifacimento, urisk, wasserman, yale**

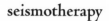
seismotherapy

(saɪzməʊ›θɛrəpɪ) [from Greek *seismos*, σεισμό-ς, shaking, + Latin *therapīa*, adapted Greek *therapia*, θεραπεία, healing] NOUN

The treatment of a disease by controlled vibrations.

(**1743** J. GINGELL & T. TOWNSHEND. *Accounts of the Thirteen Cities of Ememeer*, expanded ed.) **p 432** The fifth time the people attempted to rebuild the city of Ememeer, they selected a site slightly to the southwest, as suggested by a suavely crooning breeze. For the first few months of booming and busting moons, oscillating with the inconstant finances of light, the new Ememeer seemed a thriving place. Trade flourished, trafficking largely in spiders' silk, foreign perfumes, and gaslight, and the citizens reveled in their traditional lives of swift carriages and lavish masquerade balls lacking faces and end. And thence did the earthquakes began. The Ministers of Knowing Things speculated that surely the tremors were the work of some hidden volcano lying drowsy and dormant and drifting beneath the great marketplace, mumbling calamitous curses and shaking the city out of its own indolence. The citizens attempted to assimilate the problem, gluing vases to the mantelpieces, adding voluptuous structural supports, and making a frivolous lottery out of the number of aftershocks per interminable minute. However, as the civic officials well knew, the constant and increasingly passionate earthquakes would soon breed public discontent, and something had to be done. 'Twas soon reported that a malady was sweeping

Ememeer, afflicting the victim with infectious boredom, respiratory difficulties, and an inability to concentrate upon important business and snippy conversations regarding the neighbors' shoddy shrubberies. The pious middle-aged, especially, were suffering, as were the mercilessly gorgeous celebrities who came to function as the most elegant representatives of the afflicted. However, a prominent doctor soon reported the revelation of repeated studies—astonishingly, the best of treatments for the ailment proved in fact to be the pesky earthquakes themselves. Most helpful, indeed, proved registration in the Catalogue of the Disordered, and the purchase of expensive but worthwhile tickets to the Seismotherapy Parlours in which the aftershock were distilled into a controlled vibration to be bought and sipped in syrup form. As the epidemic increased, so too did the Parlours, and people became sicker and more pleased than before. There did remain one faction who noted that the earthworms seemed immune or otherwise unbothered, and these dissidents retreated to the wooded hills to bury their belongings and themselves in sparkling red clay. But this was a small demographic, and, the civic officials reasoned, hardly significant in the grand scheme of Ememeer and the earth.

See also **anachorism**, **caryatid**, **colubriferous**, **enantiodromia**, **fern-ticle**, **filipendulous**, **libeccio**, **seismotherapy**, **turngree**, **xenia**

selenite

('sɛlɪnaɪt) [From Latin *selēniītēs*, from Greek *selenites lithos*, σελνίτης λίθος, the moon stone or mineral gypsum, so called because its size was believed to wax and wane with the moon; from *Selene*, the goddess of the moon] NOUN

I. *Gypsum, the treasure believed to oscillate according to the lunar phase,* or, 2. *An inhabitant of the moon.*

(**1840**   J. MOOMIN.   *True Stories for very young beings*) **p 27** Fancy that! Child, there are People prancing on the moon! Who are they, these silly selenites, a-romping and a-reeling up there? Barons and shoemakers, gypsies agleam and mariners hauling their nets full of jellyfish and dreamy dust. It's your moon, child, and you can hold it in your unwashed hands and watch it swell and snore like the napping cat. And look there! the deer, bounding across the craters' crumbly cusps, with antlers of spun sugar and shadows which speak and which resemble the first letter of your name. How did they get up there, by what wavering path? And what do they do up there, with no wind to sneak up their sleeves and no sensible way to stay fixed to the floor? The moon is a comedy! The people all tell riddles, and the answer always sounds like *sea*, and the shining scars of meteors are naught but a silly tale about a dog. And there are dances, child, masquerade balls, and I will find for you one of their befeathered and bejeweled disguises so you might flicker as a dove among the fools. They play marbles in the white valleys, ninepins with the sky. On the moon there are no autumns, but always is there laughter, and though there are times the moon must grow red and solemn as a scraped knee, it has always and shall ever be a place of weightlessness and light.

See also **catabibazon**, **selenitic**

selenitic

(sɛlɪˈnɪtɪk) [From Latin *selēniītēs*, from Greek *selenites lithos*, σεληνίτης λίθος, the moon stone or mineral gypsum, so called because its size was believed to wax and wane with the moon; from *Selene*, the goddess of the moon] ADJECTIVE

1. *Containing gypsum*, or, 2. *pertaining to the moon; often said of a flower that opens in moonlight.*

(**1735** H. M. O'COURKE. *Botany Ascendant*) **p 431** But let us imagine the state of this earth, if for but a single night all flowers indulged themselves unto becoming selenitic. That night, we of the walking world would find ourselves stricken by a kind of aromatic insomnia, unconsoled and unblessed even by cool water. We would wander from the jolted stillness of our beds and into the meadows, the tame and angelic gardens, the feral, salivating woods, and on this selenitic night, there would rise the robber moon with all its perilous charisma of confectioner's dust. And all the beings of the floral kingdom would respond; the irises would unfold in all their frail eroticism, and the lilies upon the surface of the bottomless lake would sail in a confidential tide. The sunflowers would strain upwards in irony, the heliotropes towards a new lover so unlike the amorous sun, and the seed-globes of the aged dandelions would themselves rise up lunar to misdirect the moths. We ourselves would wear crowns of lilac and shoes of marigold, picking bouquets for the glamorous bats. And the eyes of daisies, eyes of day, these at last would unfold to their full astronomy, and would know more than we. No doubt such an event would prove remarkable in the history of botany, but it is likely too that scarcely would we recall the selenitic night, or otherwise would dismiss it as a dream.

See also **adelaster**, **selenite**

shiterow

(ʃɪtɪɜ:o) [from *shite*, Old English *scítan*, corresponding to early Old Frisian *skíta*, Dutch *schijten*, Modern German *scheissen*, Old Norse *skíta*, Middle Swedish *skíta*, Danish *skide*, from Old Teutonic root **skĭt**, now modern English curse word *shit*, excrement. The latter part may be a corrupt form of *heron*.] NOUN

A heron.

(**1747** Z. PROTHERA & E.M.BAYLEAF. *Chronicles of the Avian Wars,* volume V) **p 900** It did require some time to ascertain that the shiterow was in truth the heron in disguise, masking its symbolical throat behind an antiquated pseudonym. The ruse was no doubt adopted in order to spy upon the fateful negotiations and the diabolical, political, romantical trysts taking place among the waterweeds; with the intrigue now exposed, we must determine exactly how much the bird knows.

See also **chirm, engastration, kae**

spectrey

('spɛktrɪ) [from *specter*, French *spectre* (16th century, = Italian *spettro*, Spanish and Portuguese *espectro*), from Latin *spectrum*, *specĕre*, to see] NOUN

A place of specters.

(**1811** R. DARLINGTON *Grand Musæums of the Continent: A Tour*) **p 43** Should the visitor care to look to the left, there will be apparent a decidedly spooky artifact of some six hundred years ago, once a dour alchemist and now a sulfurous poltergeist with an interest in chemistry. Indeed! One cannot deny that among all musæums, our spectrey holds the most profuse and multicolored host of spirits, from deceased ballerinas twirling on imaginary toes to the eerie purrs of the mummified Abyssinian cats. Turning our gaze this way, Madame, past the broken column, I do believe you shall be most pleased to examine one "Catriona", a peculiar apparition found trilling and playing cats'-cradle with spiderwebs beside her grave upon the dusky moors. This side of the velvet ropes, please. And fear not, dear boy, for that ghoul from whom you shrink is merely a departed philosopher, with toga now reduced to transparent asbestos but still speaking of invisible things. Here is the duchess, and here her beloved wolfhound with spittle and yet no tongue; here is a knight of immense courage and dubious morality, now no more than a filmy suit of armor with a sword like an April breeze. Note the hooting of the aspiring banshee, whilst of high distinction is the spectral specimen *lemures*, as may be identified through its terrified, lunar, omniscient eyes. Madame! please do not use your umbrella to hit the specters. One must display an air of deference, a slight bow and a clear, academic interest in the ghosts, lest out of mutiny or boredom, curiosity or spite, realize they possess now that superb ability to drift through walls, and our spectrey's grand inventory escapes to scatter itself over the waking earth.

See also **idolum, lemures**

supernatant

(s(j)uːpəˈneɪtənt) [adopted Latin *supernatant*, from *super*, above, beyond + —*natant*, Anglo-Norman and Latin swimming] ADJECTIVE

Floating on the surface of a body of water.

(**1891** ROSEBLADE & GILFEATHER. *A Diary of Love among the Early Dead, and Childhood Lost*) **p 23** And it is this that I recollect best of all, with the lucidity of water and the insidiousness of miniature legs. You remember them—of course you do, we cannot forget—you must remember those insects of our breathless childhood. You must recall it—how on rounded and invisible bellies we would lie unseen and entranced, there upon the coppery banks of that river whose name was taken from a vanished native tongue. How the woods pressed right up to the shore, and through the inconstant trickery of a weeping willow the broken light gave the ripples a heightened power over us. You remember the water beetles, the water skitters, supernatant beings, those insects gliding like delicate ideas across the just at the dire edge of the undertow. And how we would catch them, wrongly certain that they did not bite, with the currents murmuring their teary nonsense around our skinned knees. You remember it, of course, how we believed in riparian nymphs but not drowning; how once the fishes taught kisses to our toes; how I swam faster than you did and how never do the water beetles quite submerge themselves entirely, in that river whose name means something I do not recall.

suint

(swĭnt) [adopted French *suint*, earlier *suing*, from *suer*, to sweat, with an indeterminate suffix.] NOUN

The grease in a sheep's wool.

(1901 W. A. CHINNERY. *Quandaries for the Modern Conversationalist*) **p 178** I have exhausted myself trying to generate possible instances in which one might have need of this word.

See also **i-hwat**, **wrancheval**

tectrix

('tɛktrɪks) [Latin *tectrix* (feminine of Latin *tector*), from *tegĕre*, to cover + *trix*, suffix analogous to English –*tress* denoting feminine agent-noun] NOUN

One of any small feathers covering the base of the quills of a bird's wing.

(**1709** S. PREEN-LIKORISH. *Times of Gravitas and of Light, with suggestions for the explorer*) **p 99** And it has occurred to me that one might take it upon oneself to wander the hundred thousand empires of the birds, from the breathless shapeshifting of the upper atmosphere to the jungle's canopy fraught with ambiguous cries, and to the rooftop where the starlings sit with sinister intent. Bearing a basket

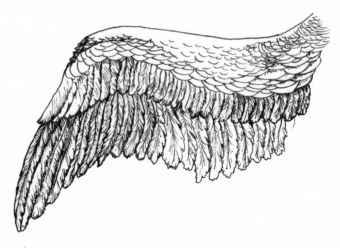

under one's arm one could begin the gathering of tectrices from the lost luculent pinions of the archaeopterae, the funeral adornments of the crows, the plumes shed from the lethal legions of the goldfinches and the sweetheart thrushes and those too of the cranes and the glorious wild turkeys, and more twilit quills taken from the wings of the mourning doves, who keep their secrets. With a single tectrix bequeathed by every bird which swoops and descends 'neath these amnesiac clouds, I calculate that by the end of the journey one would carry a burden of feathers so great that the weight of flight would surpass the heaviness of the glowing and grinding planet itself.

See also **chirm, engastration, kae, shiterow**

telarian

(ˈtɜlə(r)ɪən) [from Latin *tēla*, a web + *-ian*, suffix denoting 'of or pertaining to'] NOUN

A creature that spins a web.

(**1950** V. SKIVINGTON. *Uncertainty and the Arachnids, transcript, as presented to the Royal Society of Phobias*) **p 403** States Thomas Browne, 'we will not dispute the picture of the Telary spiders, and their position in the web'. Yet in light of the advances of subatomic physics in a swelling universe, I would submit we have ample reason to believe that spiders inhabit a plane of existence just slightly different from our own. Perhaps this pertains in some way to their multifarious optics, for like the prophet seamstresses the arachnids possess as many eyes as there are colors to be perceived, plus one unnamable hue. Yet it is as telarians that the spiders reveal their true nature, in that ritual of art inextricable from cosmological inconstants. For some theories do suggest that this universe exists only as the strings of a temporal-spatial tapestry, in which are curled a bundle of additional dimensions which we, with tears in our flawed irises, cannot comprehend: dimensions of cold fire and of water which does not slake our thirst. We subsist within the warp and the weft, and of this are we blissfully unaware. But the spiders adopt as their lifework the representation of these threads of half-substantial being: by way of their webs. And—in one of those random evolutionary jests which cause whales to walk upon vestigial submarine paws—the structures' dainty and infamous stickiness ensnares not only the iridescent gadflies and the tropical fish caught in a hapless leap; indeed, I posit, it is this gossamer art which dictates the order of reality itself. The universe is at times a wondrous orb, at times a tangle inextricable from a grand Thicket, and at other times it is a funnel with a many-handed predator waiting in its pit. The arachnid sits upon the surface of the structure, its exoskeleton remaining a part of our world, and meanwhile its eight frail legs planted lightly in the intricate Other. Remember the fact that some venoms induce in us a mad dance, and that it is in their superb strings that spiders invite other creatures to die. It may be absolutely crucial to observe that the lungs of spiders resemble books. Forthwith I shall commence to speculate upon the existence of a cosmic spinneret, the source of spacetime's mortal silk.

See also **filipendulous**

tibert

('tıbət) [adapted Flemish and Dutch *Tybert, Tibeert,* Old French *Tibert*] NOUN

A term for any cat, after the medieval allegory of Tibert, prince of cats, in the medieval allegory of Reyard the Fox. *Also utilized by Shakespeare in his character in* Romeo and Juliet, *Tybalt the cousin of Juliet, slain by Romeo.*

(**1896** M. WATKINS. *The Certain Return of the Feline, and His Schemes Rewarded*) **p 196** I have decided to call my cat Tibert. Initially, upon finding him no more than a starveling kitten, mewing and purling and bashing his disheveled blind skull beneath an upturned bucket, I had planned upon a title such as *Whiskerdum* or *Bill.* But after three and a half saucers of curdled milk my pet began to take on that gloss of pearl which burnishes certain excessively sentient things, such as elves and a few lost sorts of pearl, and at once did his eyes open wide—one emerald, one blue, dilated to drown the sunlight within. I have given him a nest formed of scullery rags, but he returned from his nocturnal jaunts of instinctive wanderlust to refuse any bed save the head of my own, and now I sleep scratched by his crowns of brambles, his sceptre paws. I glimpse him stealing along the barn's peak under the iris of the harvest moon, in pursuit of the weathervane cock; no! I cry, when he snatches my chicken and wins at the wishbone, but he is solemn and effortless as alabaster, and bites me should I try to slap his pristine nose. When I adjust my scarf and believe myself

quite fashionable in this our gilded age, I sense that stare and understand my lack of poise, and at times I survey my land with satisfaction until a subtle mew informs me that none of this truly do I own. Yes, he is a Tibert, king of cats, and I can hear his twilight duels with the wild dogs and the inconsolable, incomparable yowls of his terrible amorous trysts. Tibert is he, and he knows more than he mews. I will admit, in an undertone as I glance about and sense his nearness to my toes, that I am slightly afraid of he who is not *my* cat. Yet I have no doubt that as tonight I fall into a haze of sphinxes' dreams I will be scratching Tibert betwixt those clairvoyant ears, without needing to be asked.

See also **ailurophile**, **ycore**

transpontine

(trɑːnsˌpɒntaɪn) [from Latin *trans-*, across, beyond, over, + *pons, pont-em,* bridge + *-ine,* suffix denoting 'pertaining to' or 'of the nature of'; second connotation a transference from 'the other side of the bridges in London, i.e. south of the Thames, from the melodramatic and sensational style of drama in vogue in the 19th century at the 'Surrey-side' theatres] ADJECTIVE

1. *From the opposite side of a bridge,* or, 2. *melodramatic.*

(**1773**   L. SMYTHE-MARKHAM.   *Residency and Madness, being a warning for all sane folk and those of Good Reason*) **p 258**   It remained unknown as to why those who made their home on the other side of the river behaved in such a barbarous manner, or lack thereof. Certainly it could not have been the water; otherwise the people of the normal village would have acted with the same sort of disgraceful vulgarity, situated as they were upon the opposite banks like a burnished mirror remaking the realism of a defective world. But the river was murky and homogenous, and a dipper lowered into any given ripple would yield the same drink, shimmering still with fishes' scales and shocking one's teeth. It could be denied not, however, that those who dwelt upon the other shore were different. From the good village one could see the homes on the contrary side, which unlike their own lacked any dignity or the resolution to use right angles. There they slept in tumbledown temples, burrows with portals fuming and aglow, mud huts like the palaces of frantic swallows. In the amplification of night the people of the normal banks could catch strains of the other side's utterly pointless music, maudlin and antiquated and similar to the singing of treacle. Across the heaving waters one could glimpse their candelabras, arrayed haphazard and hazardous in the weeping willow boughs; their morose emissary fainted on a regular basis. Once, one of the people of the decent village dared wed somebody from the other side. She crossed the bridge at its most tenuous point, where cable and column became naught but cobweb, and the pair married in a shower of hops and firecrackers, as was purportedly customary among the transpontine tribes. The girl started then sloping around the streets, weeping and pounding her fists on the carriages and collapsing at the sight of mildly pretty things. She spoke only in superlatives, and consumed only blueberry pastries. And all in the good village could hear the pair fighting, screaming and throwing vases of exaggerated daisies, and then amending it all in sobs and cries like the ecstasy of dirty saints. It would seem that her hapless husband too had adopted the melodrama—mayhap they ate it, with their suppertime—and they argued all the time, even in public, and were happier than anybody else.

See also **xenia**

tremogram

(**'trɛmǝgræm**) [from Greek *tremôs*, τρέμιν to tremble, quiver + -*gram*, Greek *gramma*, γράμμα, something written, letter (of the alphabet)] NOUN

An irregularity characterizing one's handwriting.

(**1660** THE WRIT OF BANDOGS, ET AL. *Warnings for the King, in times of assassination and revolt*) **p 39** And this be how she shall triumph. Thou hast vowed for so long that never could she catch thee, and aye did thee swear'st to truly believe it, but all may discern that thou knowest it untrue. Thou hast ordered thy windows obscured, o'ercast with cloaks so gladly given by thy faithful subjects when first thou perceived that not e'en behind the crowne might thou hide. Thou hast adopted a clever nickname, a coterie of guardsmen, and a charmed çalico cat for the good luck it holdeth in its flawless paws. Thou hast taken a dagger with a scabbard of pearl. But none of it shall save thee now. For she shall seek thee out through that avenue where thou art most vulnerable: through the supernatural fragility of the word. In thy flight thou shalt cease to sign treaties, and the princesses of the southwest lands shall never again receive thy letters of eternall love, but with all thy vanity a diary shall seem harmless enough. *August 11ᵗʰ, thou shalt write, I have inspected my librarie. Works of Pliny missing unexpectedly, but I have found a book regarding th'eagles. I am safe today.* Thou shalt inscribe more, more, more unto an ache. *I crave oranges for no cause at all. A cramp strikes me; today is the anniversary of Caesar's death.* In writing, huddled in thy darkened chamber, thou wilt believe thyself secure. *Free,* thou shalt write. But in all thy clever majesty thou shall go so far as to sign thy own name. This shall be how she may find thee: that final swoop, the eely streak of thy signature's last letter, thy tremogram which so many tutors did once fight to eradicate. Thou shalt just be placing the beaded dot upon the *i* when the weight of her shadow shall as conscious fog upon the page where thou shalt have written so many meaningful things, and then shall thou know she hath caught thee at last.

See also **latitant**

tribuloid

('trɪbjʊlɔɪd) [from modern Latin *Tribulus*, after botanical genus (from *tribulus*, a caltrop or spiny weapon) + *-oid*, from Greek *eidos*, εἶδος, resemblance] ADJECTIVE

Bearing prickly or spiny fruit.

(**1765** R. M. SPRAT. *The Unvoiced Complaint, and a Demand for Justice*) **p II**   There are those of us, a tragically large sector of the population kept silent by our shame, for whom life has been not merely year after year of trials and tribulations, but also (and coextensively) year after year of trials and tribuloids.

See also **encardion**

turngree

(tɜːngriː) [from *turn*, Old English *tyrnan* and *turnian*, both adapted Latin *tornāre*, to turn in a lathe + *gree*, adapted Old French *gré* = Italian, Spanish *grado*, from Latin *gradum*, step] NOUN

A winding, spiraling stair.

(**1743** J. GINGELL & T. TOWNSHEND. *Accounts of the Thirteen Cities of Ememeer,* expanded ed.) **p 760** It remained unclear as to precisely when the turngree appeared at the center of the eleventh Ememeer, and it was the children who were the first to notice, whilst chasing through the alleyways the elusive Tibert, King of Cats. Darting among the rubbish and the mirror metropolis of the mice, they discerned upon their lithe limbs a certain mounting shadow. Though the adults of Ememeer initially dismissed the grimy reports of the children—go to your beds, they commanded, examining their fingernails with much maturity and sanitation—soon enough, they too observed the silhouette moving like a plague or a sundial's eye over the city. Perhaps the turngree's random appearance could have been overlooked, had only the structure some determinate end. But like a nautilus embedded in arithmetic, the winding stair only stretched away to be hidden by complacent clouds; even upon the sunniest of days, the eye could discern no end. At night the normally taciturn moon would briefly deviate from its path to swing in luminous nausea 'round the tower, and soon enough no citizen of Ememeer could buy or sell or slumber in the relentless knowledge of its presence. Three committees

convened to discuss what course of action might be best to take, but two so embroiled themselves in arguments that their members became petrified wood, while the last fled somewhere into the southwest to take vows of hedonistic ignorance. None could determine whether the source of the turngree might be some sort of geologic event, some highly aesthetic eruption of crystals, or if it were some sort of architectural blossom, given that it seemed to adore the rain. Some suggested the caprice of some gargantuan and silent Engineer, while to others did occur the fact that some insects have been known to cultivate the spiral within their arcane nests. 'Twas hypothesized too that the center of the turngree could be nothing save a pillar of whorled light. But nobody really desired to mount the turngree, to ascertain its ultimate height and therefore expose their throats to a star-fanged sky. Only the children dared climb it, and also the cats, both being quite interested in a greater proximity to birds.

See also **anachorism, caryatid, colubriferous, enantiodromia, fernticle, filipendulous, seismotherapy, xenia**

217

ughten

('ʊtɛn) [Common Teutonic: Old English *úhtan;* Old Saxon *ûhta,* Middle Dutch *uchten, ochten,* Old High German *ûhtâ, uohtâ,* Gothic *ūhtwō,* Old Norse and Icelandic *ótta,* Norwegian and Swedish *otta*: relationship to forms outside of Germanic is probable but uncertain] NOUN

That part of the morning just preceding daybreak.

(**1794** THIRLWALL, ASHBURNER, & MacTEAR. *The Twenty-fifth Hour*) **p 52** It is known—not only to we ourselves but also to the tearstained bats and to the swift-disintegrating tiger moths—indeed, it is known that the ughten represents a slightly different territory than that which we inhabit in the salve and scorch of sun and the heavenly torments of our sleep. In this hour there shall forever be a sort of Intermission, a pausing of the dew clinging to the underbellies of torn leaves. As the terminus of light and shade moves over the surface of this slowly moaning earth, so are we reminded that the archers and lyricists of another continent are subsiding into their twilight, that in their slumber they shall dream of our own waking agonies. Now must we face the extinction of our own ghosts. There comes a point of divestment and abandon, in which we are neither dawn nor darkness but rather the astronomic, mathematical, luminous void: neither the full selves we have so endeavored to be, nor our opposite-exacts, but the very instant of nothing between. Behind us the stars fall away, and before us the bells are awakening with heavenward cries, but in this moment we are naught, save perhaps the dissolution, the echo, and the silence.

See also **byss, vorago**

uloid

(**'ju:lɔɪd**) [from Greek *oulê*, *ουλή*, scar + ~ *oid*, from Greek *eidos*, *εἶδος*, resemblance] ADJECTIVE

Resembling a scar.

(**1899** F. HOLLOWAY. *Psychology's Underbelly: A New Science*) **p 110** This the age of modern psychology constitutes most certainly one of great advancement, already historic and already halcyon; no longer do we adhere to the old doctrine wherein sorrow is an airborne virus, and dreams are only water we cannot touch. We are confident of our present understanding of the exaggerations and the oblivions of our own brains, and now we commence the alphabetization of all possible memory. But as we must admit having now deduced the laws of neurologic honesty, there do remain some mysteries: most paramount of these might be the true *shape* of curiosity. In our labyrinthine grey matter with all its miniature minotaurs, does curiosity take the form of an acorn, or perhaps (most traditionally) of a cat? Or does inquisitiveness surround our upturned heads as does a garland of authentic ivy in amongst the broken columns? Perhaps the anatomy of curiosity is that of a boat running on and on towards an unimaginable mermaid; one of our finest microscopes has suggested that it is in fact a miniscule Specialist scurrying up and down our spine. We may find it to resemble nothing so more as the precocious evening star, if only we might vivisect our inner cranial skies. Or perhaps, as a stubbornly anonymous somebody has proposed, curiosity takes the shape of a scar. We called this absurd at first and laughed in our laboratories, but now we reconsider our doubt. If in all the dreams of fact curiosity is uloid, then we have reason to believe that all questions ooze from wounds, sting us with and linger always in a shining ache, and the desire to know is coextensive with the exploration of past pain.

See also **umbration**

umbration

(ʌmbreɪʃn) [adapted Latin *umbrātio*, from *umbrāre*, shadow] NOUN

1. *In heraldry, a faintly outlined figure,* or, 2. *an indistinct representation of something.*

(**1533** ANONYMOUS. *Bestiarium Maestitia*) **p 15** At first the Umbration be but a trembl'ng figure at that verge of what mayst we see, a slight Form that slippeth behind a silver tree with much rustles of Invisible Feetes. We shall turn from its Presence, for a time. But hence doth the Umbration drift past the window, along a passage where we dar'st not walk, and though we do pursue't to the sobbing Garden it shall disappear. Soon shall the Umbration Manifest its Being in all Places of Note, in the villages and the chapel beams, on the river's banks where Thyme doth grow and fade awaye. What doth it demand? We do shrink in our Terror, but the Umbration be but a Curious Being crown'd with æthereal scar. For aye, in truth it desireth naught save to glimpse our Art and many Politicks, and findeth the Sorcery in our Wrists. And as we do see the Umbration oft staring with a Narrow Gaze, as do the Inquisitive and Short-Of-Sight, so must we suspect that we, our enchanting and enchanted selfes, be as faint and inscrutable to the Umbration as it doth seem to us, peering upon our own Visible World.

See also **amphisbaena, barghest, bucentaur, dipsas, mamuque, pyrausta, scytale, uloid, wasserman, yale**

uræus

(jʊˈriːəs) [A Latinization of *ouraios*, οὑραῖος, originally 'of the tail,' given in the 5th century by Horapollo, one of the last leaders of the Egyptian priesthood, as the Egyptian name for the cobra] NOUN

A representation of a rearing serpent, worn by Egyptian dignitaries as a crown or circlet.

(1801   T. L MacROBBIE & F SYLVEWRIGHT, EDS. *Modern Archaeology: A Superlative Text*) **p 77** Within the grandest tombs, where the solar hieroglyphics stand stricken speechless by their own excavation, the pharaoh remains the bravest of figures. His clavicles are traced in a particular ink whose formula shall never again be known, and which shall never fade, but will burn the eye so reckless as to gaze too long upon it. His hand is a command upraised at a flawless angle, his brow wide and simple with its personal omniscience over the sands. And upon his head there sits the serpent. It is a diadem of infinite ribs, a crown of livid scales, with a head rearing up like the last sibilance of a signature. Its tongue represents choice, or treachery. In a hundred layers of encoded text, the last frail papyrus scrolls explain that it is the serpent who is the perpetual protector, following the king into the parabolic underworld to fight there that demon who takes alternately the form of the rabbit, the reed, and thirst. But the mad nomadic scholars of the dunes disagree. In their robes of jackals' hide, they insist that in spite of what we might see the pharaoh by no means wears the uræus. In truth it is the

serpent who wears the king, presiding with a small smile
over the ascent, the stony shine, and the swift collapse of
the crypts.

See also **amphisbaena, dipsas, scytale**

urisk

('ʊərɪsk) [adapted Gaelic *ùruisg, uirisg*] NOUN

A supernatural being said to inhabit lonely places.

(1951 H. POMFREY. *Sad Revisions of the Bestiary*)
p 731 As the human population upon this drowsy earth
multiplies and swells, so must the quantity of lonesome
places proportionately shrink. There remain few ashen
hilltops which have not felt the weight of a human
footprint, and rare is the grove or the moaning shore
where one cannot hear the ambient din of distant traffic,
the lethally marvelous machine. Our airplanes have eyes,
and objectives. In ages past, when the aureate straw of
thatched roofs would be regularly swept into space and the
bamboo of bridges still whistled riddles over the waters
and the lions still roamed gypsy over the eight continents,
loneliness possessed still its definite loci. Between town
and luminous town, past footpath and safe haven and seedy
port, there remained the midst of the black meadows,
lachrymose moors, the forests and inland seas of the night.
And in the endless dusk of empty places—therein dwelt
the urisks, each alone and reveling in the golden age of
forlorn voicelessness, meditating upon notions forever
undisclosed. But our species approaches now its victory
in its diligent and militant and artistic crusade against
the dark; as our factories spread their cancerous warmth,
infectious convenience, and our settlements reproduce
themselves with incestuous shops, and our asphalt conceals

pothole and anthill and petrified fern alike, there remain
fewer and fewer points upon this earth which one can
call truly lonely. We are hoping to be everywhere. As
such, the urisks are forced increasingly to concentrate and
consolidate themselves in whatever locales they can find,
though even the fantasies of the Sahara and the intimate
crevices of the rainforests stand naked now to the hosts
of contrails up above. Desperate now, the urisks drift in
shock across the surface of the seas, where at least the lungs
of the dying waves seem not to bother them. And so the
ghosts, in all their multitudes flocking to the globe's last
pockets of seclusion, can in fact never be relieved of one
another's company. In such infinite presence, solitude is
absent.

See also **amphisbaena, barghest, dipsas, disomus, mamuque,
pyrausta, scytale, umbration, wasserman, yale, ythe**

vademecum

('vɑːˌdeɪˌmeɪkəm)   [Latin, *vāde* imperative singular of *vādĕre* to go + *mēcum* with me]   NOUN

A book suitable for carrying on one's person.

(**1796** COLE & HUDSON. *A History of Paragraphs up to this point, with improved punctuation and intimations of Beyond*) **p 162** There was a time we each carried our own amulet of words, a personal and precious book we would hold to our breasts as egrets hold their baskets of cloud. At times, when drunk on amber or in a tumult of acrobatic love, we would share with one another these volumes: some of us bore those tales we choose to name as fact, and walked with a convoy of twittering footnotes to guide us in everyday affairs. And there were those readers of epical dullness, embracing with pride their procedural manuals regarding barrel-making, and those who gnawed restless upon volumes of dubious cookery. The diarists swung pocket-sized odes to themselves upon chains of false brass, while simple biographers wept with longing for their long-lost subjects. Others clutched our most cherished novels and thereby could never be lonely and yet never consoled, aching over the fatal flaws of doomed heroines. Some of us dangled o'er pounding breasts our own little codices of poetry whose rhymes functioned as unreliable maps, though dictionaries loudly cursed their bearers to eternal meandering among the baleful trees. Yet inevitably did novelty fade, commerce necessitating a swifter life unburdened by paper and plot; the vademecum became obsolete. Or so we believed, for a time. Recently, however, a kind of weak trilling against our sternums has given us reason to believe that each of us walks still weighted and elevated by a vademecum, a book invisible as instinct, disloyal as a cuckoo's promises, insidious as the wind beneath the door.

See also **chorizont, refacimento, scytale**

ventilow

(ˈvɛntɪlo) [apparently adapted Italian *ventola*] NOUN

A fan.

(**1729** LADIES OF THE COURT OF EDINBURGH. *The Language of Accessories*) The Lady spreads her arms. She lowers her fan to bare, moonstone toes, wrist all a-shiver, then swift does she upraise it with a sweep like saltwater. *The king,* says she in silence, *is dead indeed.* Hand fluttering as do the infant sparrows in their descent towards ash, she bends to indicate now that *aye, but the princess has escaped to the cold north.* A pace to the left, and thus may one know that the sinister tryst shall be held in a bower of roses, and admittance granted only when wearing a mask. But already her face is nothing save disguise. *I desire to betray,* say her whetted fingernails. *And in ecstasy to be betrayed.* Mouth subtle as silk, the Lady curves her rhythmic spine as if in exultation. *I will have no mercy, and I am not what I am.* She turns, beckoning towards that pit where shining clavicle meets its ending beneath the throat, and then unfolds that quivering ventilow to its broadest span in the best imitation of a wing, and hides her painted eyes, that we might know all she has said.

See also **latitant, tremogram**

versipellous

('v ɜːrsɪpɛləs) [from Latin *versipell-is*, from *vertĕre*, to turn + *pellis*, skin] ADJECTIVE

Having the quality of changing skin.

(**1939**   G. W. WINDUS, ED.. *Formulae of Being*) **p 223** Within the octopus, specialized cells with specialized names respond to the outcries of the nervous system, as the celebrant responds to a drumbeat, so that in times of fright, of hunger, of love's spontaneous and dangerously hilarious convulsion, the organism alters its hue to take on the look of that-which-is-something-else.   Thenceforth, however, the being of the camouflaged beastie comes into question.   Consider now the octopus: ambidextrous assassin clutching eight submerged worlds, tentacles flickering from the slate of the seafloor to the bloodied color of the coral wilderness.   We shall not dispute the transformation of the octopus, by any means, but we shall dispute its character.   For what does it mean, when a creature takes on the role of being different than that which it is, or was, or ought to be? A formula:

1.   That which a being is-not will be different from that being.
2.   If a being looks different from itself, it is different from itself.
3.   The octopus looks different from itself.
4.   Thus, the octopus is what it is-not.

We do accept the possibility that our logic may not be as

logical as we profess it to be. But what is it that makes us other than the octopi? We scrutinize our own translucent fingerprints.

See also **i-hwat**, **inquiline**, **vespertilionize**

vespertilionize

(vɛspə(r)tɪliənaɪz) [from Latin *vespertīlio*, bat + *-ize*, Latin *–īzāre*, Greek *ίζειν*, suffix designating verbs] VERB

To turn into a bat.

(**1905** H. HESPEROS. *Confessions of a Nocturnal Wench, or, the Airborne Diary*) **p 127** And what drives me to it? It isn't for the blood of it, the sucking and the sensuous gore of crystalline teeth upon a maiden's frenzied jugular; I possess blood enough threatening now to burst from within my anguished veins, when too high I ascend towards Cassiopeia's voided heart. Nor is it for that moment of terrible humanity, when returned to a woman's form I fall to my restored knees after a murderous night of frail and airborne claws. It isn't even for the shrieking sake of flight, nor even for the auditory sight of a lovestruck moth given existence only by the shape of its own echo. But all addictions have their secret motive, for the melancholic opium-eater with her bundle of lotuses, and aye, for me as well. I vespertilionize not for the being of a bat, order *Chiroptera*, and not for the vacillating wisdom of *Homo sapiens*, but for that riveting and remaking moment of nothing between, the body nameless and without form—not woman, not bat, but the very pulsating *between* embracing each at once.

See also **ughten, versipellous**

virgula

('vɜːgjʊlə) [Latin *virgulā*, a small rod or twig, or a critical mark, diminutive of *virga*, twig, rod, wand] NOUN

1. *one of the spines of a stingray*, or, 2. *a divining rod, the* virgula divina *often used by miners to find gold or silver*, or, 3. *a slash / used as a comma in medieval manuscripts*, or, 4. *One of ten musical notes utilized in medieval written music*, or, 5. *The axis, said to resemble a quill pen, of a fossilized member of the genus of simple organisms* Hydra, *noted for their apparent absence of biological aging unto death.*

(**1874** O. BLACKBURN. *The Tome Unread*) **p 321** Now do I hold in broken hand the virgula; this is its absolute lightness, insubstantial as a notion and intricate as the fingerprint. This is its symmetry, and this is how it is within me. And as Sir Thomas Browne informed me, two hundred improbable years ago, *studious observers may discover more analogies in the book of nature, and cannot escape the elegancy of her hand.* Yes, certain structures recur and names repeat, thoughts reappearing in a new body only to depart, and the words reinvent themselves only to rupture against the substance of the world, and the story must happen to us all over again.

See also **catacoustics, lemniscus**

vorago

(vɒˈreɪgəʊ) [Latin *vorāgo*, from *vorāre*, to devour] NOUN

An abyss.

(**1927** S. ALLDREAD. *Holes currently present in our Knowledge: the absent Fact*) One would think that the vorago would have been detected earlier, as vast and as vacuous as it is. Even traumatic millennia ago, geographic sages were plotting a voluptuous equator on the inside of tortoiseshells, and mariners have calculated longitude's own backbone though signal fires blinking between Gibraltar and the Solomon Sea; conquerors have plotted the finest transoceanic courses from empire to exploration to profitable extermination. Now do we possess aeroplanes like dragonflies in hysteria, wings doubled and propellers abuzz. One would have expected at least some hint from the amateur aviatrixes, in their balloons with bellies of flame, but these return bearing no news save the dusty propaganda borne upon stratospheric winds. Unwittingly lost, we believed that such a presence as the vorago could only absent be. But by definition, one supposes, wilderness shall be those regions whose details are not drawn, sites where upon parched maps of centuries past one would have found only the amnesiac dragons of *incognita*, and where on the charts of centuries to come one will find the dragons once again. We discovered it only through the helpful directions of a certain half-starved and feline wild child whose eyes were pupils in their entirety. She pointed

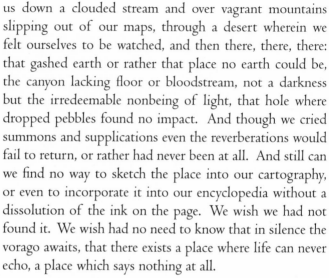

us down a clouded stream and over vagrant mountains slipping out of our maps, through a desert wherein we felt ourselves to be watched, and then there, there, there: that gashed earth or rather that place no earth could be, the canyon lacking floor or bloodstream, not a darkness but the irredeemable nonbeing of light, that hole where dropped pebbles found no impact. And though we cried summons and supplications even the reverberations would fail to return, or rather had never been at all. And still can we find no way to sketch the place into our cartography, or even to incorporate it into our encyclopedia without a dissolution of the ink on the page. We wish we had not found it. We wish had no need to know that in silence the vorago awaits, that there exists a place where life can never echo, a place which says nothing at all.

See also **abature, anachorism, byss, catacoustics, cosmognosis, jornada**

wangrace

(wangreɪs) [from *wan-*, a prefix expressing privation or nega-
tion, from Old English and Old German, Old Norse *—van*, and
grace-, adapted French *grâce*, from adapted Lating *grātia*, pleas-
ing quality, attractiveness, or goodwill, or gratitude; 'gruel' taken
from Scottish and Anglo-Irish dialect] ADJECTIVE, or, NOUN

1. *ungraceful*, or, 2. *a type of gruel.*

(**1836** B. J. FETTIPLACE. *Life Among the Oats Continued
Yet Again: Elmer Reaches Ninety*) **p 347** As he grew older,
and correspondingly more cantankerous, Elmer joined
that school of philosophy which is associated with the
quintessence of Porridge. In a great spill of luck had he
stumbled upon that most canonical book of the theory
of breakfast, *Doxia Brosia* (1604), wherein he read the
monumental declaration: "wee shall finde within our warm
and swyrling bowles the shades, the tastes, the secrets
of the Universe ytself." As Elmer saw it, however, there
could exist only two species of hot cereal which might
be considered Universal; their recipes remained highly
hypothetical and expressible only in higher math, but the
idea was logical as a tablespoon, nonetheless. The first
truly cosmic cereal might be that Immaculate Porridge,
whose ingredients represented the pinnacle of culinary
poise, the perfect ratios of grains and milk, raisins and
a treasure-trove of brown sugar. The existence of this
Porridge would indicate that the heavens are governed by
the principle of scrumptiousness: this is an expanding

sphere of sweet elegance, wherein stars are intermixed with galaxies of luminous, infinitely stirring oats, and gravity manifests itself as a proportionate function of brown sugar. On the other hand, the morning meal of this firmament might well be the Wangrace. Somewhere, in some scummy celestial café or beneath the table of a stellar kitchen, there may exist a cracked cauldron in which a most disturbing substance is growing lumpy and cool. In this repugnant gruel, all ingredients are stirred into a war for mucky dominance, and there have been added constituents which ought never to have seen the light of a stove: breeds of piss, garlic with its multiple rotted hearts, mayonnaise drawn from the seas. If it is the case that our reality is manifested in the form of the Wangrace, Elmer realized, then this is a universe of chaos and distaste, a graceless vacuum of brunch wherein drift certain unidentified morsels which we decidedly do not wish to encounter. Recently, he had suspected this to be the case, but perhaps it was only indigestion.

See also **ecuelle**

wasserman

(wɒzə(r)man) [adapted German *wassermann*, literally 'water-man'] NOUN

A sea monster partially in the shape of a man, known to lay ships to waste.

(**1533** ANONYMOUS. *Bestiarium Maestitia*) **p II** We depart to fight the Wasserman, and we daren't go unarmed. For we hath heard those Horrors of the Lost Galleon, as tolden by the survivors whose near-drown'd skin hath turned entirely as Weed-of-Sea. Aye, say they, the Wasserman arisen from the waters in a spray which smothered a Star. So do we traverse the shores where doth the Forests burn, and the harbors of the fishes' Laments, and the Sands where drifteth the Filth we want no more. Board we the Ship with the great Arrows craft'd to murder then the fearfull whales, and to stab the ocean-beasts through Unknown Lung till they be dragged to the deck, and so the people laugh at the Herrings of the Nets, who glowen as they Die. Our Waste is throwen to the Deeps, and there be little we cannot defeat. But the Waves seem now to disappear, and the Wasserman appeareth not unto our sight. Unafeared be we, for sure we know that as our swordes and sails and smoke move swift o'er the waters to o'ertake the gyrdle of the globe, there shall be no Deliverance for the Wasserman.

See also **amphisbaena**, **barghest**, **bucentaur**, **dipsas**, **mamuque**, **porraceous**, **pyrausta**, **scytale**, **urisk**, **yale**, **ythe**

watchet

(wɒtʃɪt) [adapted Old French *wachet*] NOUN, or, ADJECTIVE

1. *A type of blue,* or, 2. *a cloth of this color.*

(**1751** N. GOODFELLOW. *The Aesthetic Improbable*) **p 73**
Like the quandary of the chicken and its fabulous egg, it
remains unclear as to whether the word preceded the color,
or if it was upon the weaving of a single cloak that *watchet*
was created. For who ran a razor over that apprehensive
lamb, who drew the dyes from the crushed herbs? Who
soaked the thread, and who sat at that crystalline spinning
wheel, and who caressed the loom with its gentle crone's
moans? Who wore that first cloak of purest watchet,
peering at the reflection smirking in the world of mirrors?
We can picture it now: that cloudless afternoon that Blue
donned the dusky fruit of all its labors, and feeling itself
in the garment celestial, wove itself a name.

See also **coquelicot, porraceous, porphyrogenite, xanthopsia**

wlonk

(oʊlɒnk) [Old English *wlanc*, from Old Saxon ʒ*ewlencan*, to pride oneself] ADJECTIVE

1. *proud and haughty*, or, 2. *splendid*, or, 3. *rich in sap.*

(**1873** C. L. MILLICAN-MADINE. *An Rapt Evaluation of the Theatre, in our time and Others*) **p 29** And what finer word could I possibly find to encapsulate the actress as she is? When she dons her dress whose skirts conceal an entire zodiac of legs, and the rouge which renders her a damson and a danger, and when she flaps her fan like a swansong, all may see me as I join helplessly the mass of the motionless, the faceless, the speechless throng. In the ardor of a spotlight concentrated solely upon her face, her brow gleams with a sweat as thick and golden as a slow realization, and taking her bow her hair tumbles from its excruciating pins, and I am so certain that the scintillation of her wrist, there, represents my own tale she brings now to its most supreme of conclusions—until the next night I return, bearing bouquets to bombard her unto bruises. I am not so thrown into oblivion as to forget that all she can perceive of me remains these duplicitous opera glasses; I am only two of the glassy and fixed stars here in my darkened seat. How obviously does she reach a breathless zenith I may empirically know nobody has previously achieved, as each instant she opens the marzipan of her painted mouth, and repeats those lines I have so yearned to hear: *You are seen*, she recites. *You are heard.* And how for her recurrent

and explosive death, the ruby syrup coursing from her
ersatz wounds, and the grace with which somehow she rises
from the stage to speak again. Who is she, that she can
hold me so? I know of no name beyond her immemorial
scripts and heartbreaking pantomimes, and I confess, yes, I
am incapable of conceiving her beyond the roles of all my
possible loves. And so perhaps I ought speak no further,
save to cast a limelight over the fact that it remains she, and
she alone, who can with each interminable act redefines the
meaning of what it is to be *wlonk*.

See also **homœoteleuton**, **jornada**, **jumelle**, **nubivagant**, **ventilow**

wranchevel

(**pronunciation unknown**) [occurring only in the first of the seven poems of William of Shoreham, circa 1615, wherein he writes, 'þe fend hyt was þat schente hyt al Myd gyle and hys abette, Wranchevel.'] UNKNOWN

An Old English word whose meaning remains obscure.

(**1928** PUNCH & CUMBERPATCH. *A Catalogue of Interesting Rubbish*) **p 512** Admittedly, at this point in history of English with its salivating vowels, its garden of stolen posies and synonyms for *red*, *wranchevel* makes no sense at all. But the zoological world has shown that evolution is the way of all things. It all may come down to natural selection (and, you dear and doleful critics, impugn us not as mere mooncalfs). A meaning shall arise, we understand, and if ill-suited to its environment of predatory fables, it will die out. Should some clawed connotation prove most advantageous to *wranchevel's* survival, allowing it to catch hares and burrow into tawny riverbanks with connotative claws, then that meaning will survive and reproduce itself, unto library and quill and love letter and tongue. And the pressures of subsisting within the ecosystem of whispers will then push the word into developing a meaning with teeth, with scrolled wings and hypersexual scents, for it is only mutation that maintains the life of sign and organism. Failing to evolve, the word will enter a point of stasis and remain identical to itself alone, 'til it must die and may be consigned to earth, alongside the fossilized wishbone and the noiseless trill of the last phosphorescent archaeopteryx.

See also **adelaster, bocstaff, coquelicot, homœoteleuton, holophanerous, i-hwat, yepsen**

241

xanthopsia

(zænθəʊpsiə) [from Greek *xantho-*, ζανθο, yellow + Latin *opticus*, Greek ὀπτικος, pertaining to the eye] NOUN

A condition wherein all things appear yellow.

(1891   M. RUTHERFOLD. *Pathology of Pulchritude*)   p 45   Subsequent to epical digestive wars and rhythmic fevers wracked by apparitions of canaries, the victim awakens with eyesight rendered rancorously acute, and tinted unanimously in shades of butter.   The world appears jaundiced, waspish, dandy-leonine, pissed-upon and citreous, sugared and brightly sour. The good doctors of the royal court explain that such cases find their caustic source in the mischief and pups' mayhem of certain celestial events, or a butterfly's bite, the bilious work of lemon-borne bacteria or the sinful overindulgence and private pleasure of a sunburn. Yet though to xanthopsia's splayed sufferers we offer pity, bedrest and medicines of ivory, cologne, and song, but are refused; we suffer not, they say. We simply see.

See also **bradypeptic, coquelicot, decumbiture, diapente, porphyrogenite, porraceous, watchet**

xenia

('zi:nɪə) [Latin, adapted Greek ζενία, state or relation of a guest, from ζενος, guest] NOUN

Pollination by foreign seed.

(**1743** J. GINGELL & T. TOWNSHEND. *Accounts of the Thirteen Cities of Ememeer,* expanded ed.) **p 321** Yet another century slid by with the chirrup of a southwest breeze, and so 'twould have seemed that the people of the twelfth city of Ememeer had at last repelled the danger. For it is known that the invasion of alien seed leads inevitably to pandemonium: when daisies are sown with acorns, the resulting vines are as savage as gryphons in heat, and crawl across the worm-glimmering meadows upon nervy green feet. A man impregnated by the Dog Star's glow will give birth to an infant with silver fur and a wolf's operatic instincts; a woman who copulates with firelight will never again taste anything save paprika. Thus did the people of Ememeer enclose their city in a dome of blown glass and cathedral brick, admitting neither starlight nor seed. Not the sperm of dolphin and not the kernels of corn out of other continents and not the inquisitive ova of owls—no xenia could descend upon bright Ememeer. What the people had recollected not, however, was the problem of reciprocity. All things remain always in a vehement and romantic dialectic, often with broken glass. Thus, while the townspeople had certainly guarded themselves against the siege of unknown germs, they had considered not the opposite. But upon one overheated and melting night, as a hundred thousand citizens tossed in their nightmares of jackals and irredeemable visions of possible lovers, the true nature of xenia became clear. For 'twas then that above the city's rooftops a hundred thousand faint apparitions could be glimpsed rising above the streets, mermaids and absurdities and monsters as written in pollen—and so did the reveries depart from Ememeer, with all the wanderlust of imaginary things. And the land received them. The dreams of the city drifted away from their helpless slumberers, settling uncomfortably amongst the pastures and the poplars and the stagnant ponds, and at once were new things born.

See also **anachorism, canicular, colubriferous, enantiodromia, fern-ticle, filipendulous, seismotherapy, turngree**

xenodochium

(zɛnəˈdɒkɪəm)   [Latin *xenodochīum*, adapted Greek ζενοδοχεῖον, from ζενος, stranger +δέχεσθαι, to receive]
NOUN

A guest house or hostel for the reception of strangers.

(**1817** PUNCH & CUMBERPATCH. *On Being an Excellent Host, with recipes and paragons to be imitated*) **p 152** The inn represented—in fact manifested, replete with cupola—the absolute height of luxury. The place was crafted with the idea that upon arrival one would feel no longer a stranger, but a member of an ageless aristocracy; one could for a time forget the journey's grit between teeth, with that special power of oblivion only lavishness can grant. As a visitor, one would be met firstly by the concierge, a four-armed

prodigy of servitude: all maids and grave butlers attended without wavering, without weariness, without question. The carpets would forever shine with the arrogance of velvet, mandatorily replaced each noontime. There were newly invented and scientifically scrumptious dishes, musical pastries and the soup of oranges stolen from other people's memories, all served by an invisible and discreetly levitating waitstaff. Each chamber was named for a different exotic seductress, permeated with myrrh and heaped with pillows to such a depth that one who slumbered could sink into a perpetually replenished sea of silk, traversed by lovemaking fish. And toothbrushes came gratis, bristled with dodo's feathers, and the ice was specially sculpted to represent one's most forbidden paramour. And it was vowed that no request, no matter the excess, would ever be denied. All things seemed impeccably prepared, but the trouble with intent is the fact that nothing can be thwarted like a purpose. So it was that when the visitors arrived, extravagance turned traitorous tail on the inn. For having been indulged to such a degree, they elected to wander no more among the thickets and the snakes, taking permanent residence in ultimate comfort. The hotel's doors are closed now, barred by satin rope—but from the rosy glint of laughter and the champagne toasts we still visible upon the balconies, and from the exhausted maids glimpsed napping in the windows, one can see that within the xenodochium the life of luxury slopes onward, languid, spoiled rotten, forever unspoiled.

See also **froust**

xoanon

('zəʊənɒn) [from Greek ζόανον, related to ζύειν, to scrape, carve.] NOUN

A crude image of a deity, carved of wood.

(**1884** R. LENIHAN. *Spirituality of the Miniscule*) **p 731**
Since its classical promenades and first idyllic experiments, biology has always known the termites—class *Insecta*, order *Isoptera*, nicknamed ant-of-pearl—to be among the most organized and hungry of all the creatures of this particular planet. Within a termite mound, there dwell soldiers, workers, queens and surrogate empresses, the custodians of tiny fungal workshops, saints on ravenous crusade. Their corridors remain uncharted, defying the meaning of space as we had defined it. When the termite armies devour our houses and best armchairs, they communicate their splendid strategies of hunger in a complex language of perfumes and tender vibrations not yet stolen by the English tongue. We had estimated the termites' lives to be nothing save a scramble of bellicose feeding, but now we have discovered the xoanons. For within their gritty nests, there stand the great statues—immense, in entomological and metaphysical terms—of the divine Insect, with omniscient oaken eyes and ten thousand limbs and wings of flightless mystery; around this they cluster, and to this they offer up their sawdust. And so we come to understand that the termites' size has forever belied their mammoth devotion.

See also **holophanerous, kermes, kantikoy, limax**

yale

(jeɪl) [adapted Latin *ealē*, from the Roman naturalist Pliny's *Natural History*] NOUN

A mythic horse with tusks.

(**1533** ANONYMOUS. *Bestiarium Maestitia*) **p 9** Many be our Speculations of what might we craft of the Yale's Ivorie, perhaps a Dulcimer which shall summon the Snakes or a Medicinal Potion which sings, or a Figure of great worth for a Token of Love. Voyagers of Immense Boldness do say that in the far Antipodes, where South doth forget the North, there reign'd a Queen of Terrible Ornament, upon whom euen the Eagles dare'd not flie aboue. The Queen kept among her Court a herd of Yales, fed 'pon Cat's Milk and most superb Whey. With them she slept in beds of day's-eyes flowers that they might ne'er dream, perfum'd her beastes and award'd them high place among her chiefs. And when she harvest'd the

Ivorie of the Yales, in much Blood and screams and joyous Harmonies, the statues carv'd there from could be looked upon only through the Light gaven by a Rubie. When the Southern Queen did die, so did she gather the tuskless Yales about her, and as she did fade into the Abysse where we be permitted neither Speech nor Thoughts, she did gaze into their sunken eyen, and could understand not how be it the Yales didst not adore her as she had so ador'd them.

See also **adelaster, amphisbaena, barghest, bucentaur, colubriferous, dipsas, mamuque, pyrausta, scytale, urisk, vorago, wasserman**

ycore

(i'cɔə(r)) [Old English ȝecoren, past participle from céosan, or ȝecéosan, i-cheose, to choose] ADJECTIVE, or, UNKNOWN

1. *Lovely, comely, beautiful,* or, 2. *chosen,* or, 3. *in Middle English, used as a meaningless tag for the purposes of rhyme.*

(**1677** E. YSEULT. *Philosophia Oudenia,* first edition) **p 300** From all exquisite things for which the name does cry, here upon this weary sphere of ash, stair, and gasping door, 'tis the chin of a cat—that which it is—of all things, most ycore.

See also **garguill, zumbador**

yepsen

('jɛps(ə)n) [Middle English ȝespon, ȝyspon, yepsen, corresponding to Middle Low German gespe, gepse, (göpse), Low German gepse, geps, göpse, göps (German gäspe).

Other formations found in Low German dialects, göppsche. göpske, göppelsche, early Flemish gaspe, gaps, Dutch dialect gap(e, Low German gâpske, gäppelsche. With present evidence it is impossible to determine the relationship to Lithuanian ziùpsnis = as much as can be seized with two or three fingers, a small handful.] NOUN

Two hands cupped together to form a small bowl, or the amount that may be there contained.

(**1767** L.H. COFFIN & R. DOORBAR. *The Origins of Munificent Words, in English*) For so did we require a single sign to connote both: I. that moment of complete and utter unawareness that accompanies the quenching of thirst, and 2. the immense generosity which is this world.

See also **ætites, gelatia, kirn, naricorn**

251

yleof

(ˈiːlœf) [Old English ʒeléof = Middle High German geliep: from léof, beloved or precious] NOUN

A pair of lovers.

(**1791**   F. DIMBLEBY.   *The Grammar of Criminal Loves*) **p 99**   Note *yleof*'s elegant tumble into a plural noun, a phenomenon achieved most consummately by the chattering mice and the sheep and the deer with all their tessellated fear, who in the barns and the shimmering fields and the amorous forests we glimpse mating and in spasms losing all vigilant sense: for a moment enduring only as euphoria, as realization, as anatomy and anguish and one another—these, the vastest of wildernesses within the Milky Way.

See also **i-hwat, quicquidlibet**

ythe

(i:th) [Old English *ȳþ* strong feminine, also *ȳþe* weak feminine
= Old Saxon *ūðia*, Old High German *undea, unda* (Middle High
German *unde,* **ünde**), Old Norse *unnr, uðr.*] NOUN

A wave upon the sea.

(**1707** E. RANNEY, & ANONYMOUS, ED. *The Endings
to come, as reported by Lady Ranney, midwife of Norfolk now dead*)
p 801 'Tis difficult for us to imagine, now, but the day
shall come when there remain no waves upon the sea. Now
do we wade in the rhymed and slightly revised repetitions of
the surf, calling upon the currents for our voyages o'er the
horizon towards lands of tangerines. E'en we permit our
hearts to mimic sailboats. But soon enough the ythes we
know shall no longer exist. Perhaps it shall simply be that
the oceans reach an exhaustion ten thousand leagues deep,
and care no longer to raise their united voice. Mayhap the
possible dragon which prowls the seaweed shall someday
cease its heaving, or perhaps the departure of the keening
moon shall finally leave the oceans at rest. And the waves
shall disappear, and the sole motion to witness upon the
surface of the sea will be the ripples emanating from the lips
of whales, emerging for but one moment of exhilaration.
The oceans shall be as green mirrors, beguiling the clouds
with their own transfiguring images and blinding the sun
with its own petrified face. By desolate night the seekers
of driftwood shall o'erflow with heartbreak, forced to gaze
fully upon two spheres of stars: that of the sky above,

threaded with migrating gulls, and the celestial seas below traversed by the luminous and toxic jellyfish. In tearful silence, drowning shall correspond precisely to unrequited love, and e'en shall the very last memories of the waves remain in the hushed exhalations of seashells alone.

See also **bucentaur, homœoteleuton, holophanerosis**

ziczac

(ˈzɪkzæk) [Ultimately adapted Arab *zaqzāq, saqsaq*] NOUN

An Egyptian species of plover, Pluvianus ægyptius, *which by its cry warns the crocodile of approaching danger.*

(**1881** G. GRAVES. *Shores we have not visited, and lotus-dreams thereupon*) **p 377** But how do the ziczac and the crocodilian *feel* about one another? Is there a kind of desire in their claws, absurd and unattainable, just as the screaming clock secretly longs for its own pair of swift little feet and at its core the apple lusts after the sea? For as microbes and mammals and lingering dinosaurs, this life that lives us is one of tooth and holy defecation and sex and soil and always decay, and like the quizzical plover and the devious reptile, we are not so separate as punctuation would have us believe. Of course—how could it be otherwise?—of course our story is a romance.

See also **inquiline, yleof**

zumbador

(zʊmbədɔːr) [adapted Spanish, from *zumbar*, to hum] NOUN

A hummingbird.

(**1923** E. MAJORANA, ED. *Time and Bruises*) **p 345** We realize, now, that those certain tiny creatures who possess heartbeats swifter than our own inhabit a timeline vastly different from that in which we dwell. The pulse, of course, has always consisted of beat and pause, systole and diastole, ellipsis and elaboration, but the speed of blood may in fact transform the life of a being within its spacetime; thus in our sight do the tropical fish and the lucent moths grow older with a swiftness that seems so pitiless to us. Yet they and their arteries think in and thus wholly inhabit a different timeline from our own, so they cannot possibly notice its speed, and should one observe carefully, they grow lovelier in matters of minutes and exist unburdened by memoriam. Let us consider the zumbador: let us watch its wings, the green razors of the sublunary sphere. As the sweet-pea heart of the hummingbird throbs at a rate of some eighty times per agonizing minute, so does the creature itself perceive each instant as a function of its own transience: thus is this eternity. Indeed, the universe which the zumbadors experience is so small, so brief, so breakable as to be contained within a teaspoon or a honeysuckle bloom, and the precise way time feels to a hummingbird is something unfathomable to us, extraordinary and ordinary, fleeting and forever fatal, impeccable.

See also **corbicula, telarian, ycore**

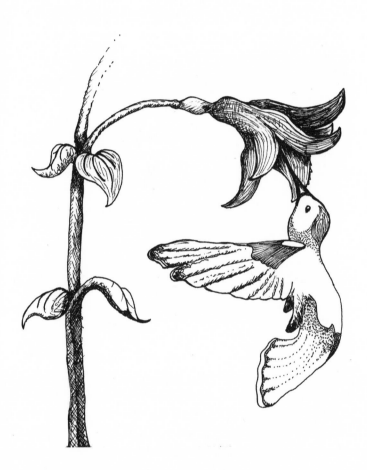

Appendix A:
a small history of the English Language, in which the isle of Britain is trounced several times, many villages are burnt, and a poet mourns for Love

The recorded history of this book—and take care, Dear Reader, against the mischief of sinister (so to speak) paper cuts—in fact begins perhaps two thousand years ago, giving or taking a few centuries and some quite gruesome battles. This would be the age in which the grand old Roman Empire, spewing rhetoric from its chariots and bearing plumes upon its head, withdrew its rule from the somewhat unruly island of Britain and proceeded to be sacked. One might have expected the populace of native Britons (the people of glorious iron weaponry, among other things, as well as the existentially dubious but poetically ever-powerful King Arthur, and also words such as *London* and *crag*) to thereafter rule their own rainy dominion with little trouble save that of the occasional belligerent dragon.

But hence began a rather exciting era for the isle, wherein the Britons found themselves overrun with the invasion of a goodly number of Germanic tribes sailing out of swampy Denmark: the Angles and Saxons (hence *Anglo-Saxon*), the Jutes, and a few Frisians (hence very few popular words). Few records of their day-to-day, epic-to-epic language remain (though they did leave such lingering tidbits as *be* and *water*) before the arrival of Christian missionaries, carrying holy water, the idea of archbishops, and Latin. Thereupon the Old English of the Anglo-Saxons, now mingled (with the natural fluidity of good conversation) with Briton and the classical tongue, was written down in sundry histories and a few inscrutable poems.

One may consult, for instance, the decaying whimsies of the tenth century *Book of Exeter*, a codex of verses and riddles compiled by a cunningly anonymous scribe. Whilst a goodly number of its puzzles concern certain lewd anatomical matters and dangling organs, out of reverence for the esteemed Reader here shall be presented solely the less bawdy twenty-seventh riddle:

Ic wiht

geseah   wundorlice

hornum

bitweonum   huþe

lædan,

lyftfæt leohtlic,   listum

gegierwed,

huþe to þam ham   of

þam heresiþe;

walde hyre on þære

byrig   bur atimbran,

searwum asettan,   gif hit

swa meahte.

Ða cwom wundorlicu

> wiht   ofer wealles hrof,
> seo is eallum
> cuð   eorðbuendum,
> ahredde þa þa
> huþe   ond to ham
> bedraf
> wreccan ofer willan—
> gewat hyre west þonan
> fæhþum feran,   forð
> onette.
> Dust stonc to
> heofonum, deaw feol on eorþan,
> niht forð gewat.   Nænig siþþan
> wera gewiste   þære
> wihte sið.

As the dear Reader might surmise, the language of Old English appears at this point utterly crackbrained or at least foreign, and would hardly be suitable conversation at a glittering modern gala. Duly translated, one reads:

> I saw a wonderful creature carrying
> Light plunder between its horns.
> Curved lamp of the air, cunningly formed,
> It fetched home its booty from the day's raid
> And plotted to build in its castle if it could,
> A night-chamber brightly adorned.
> Then over the east wall came another creature
> Well known to earth-dwellers. Wonderful as well,

It seized back its booty and sent the plunderer home
Like an unwilling wanderer. The wretch went west,
        Moved morosely and murderously on.
    Dust rose to the heavens, dew fell on earth--
        Night moved on. Afterwards no one
In the world knew where the wanderer had gone.

And what might be this wanderer? Here shall be permitted a moment in which the careful Reader may mask this page with one thoughtful hand, or perhaps pace the room and nibble an evocative cookie whilst contemplating a possible answer. As the moment has now passed, the answer shall be revealed to be the Moon, or *mōna*, as the nameless scribe would have cackled in Old English.

Perhaps the Anglo-Saxons might have continued to chant interminable hymns and tell one another riddles as nightly entertainment for centuries untold. But in the next chapter (quite a thrilling one, with many swordfights, curses, and large axes) those incorrigible Viking raiders arrived, pilfering land, livestock, and unfortunate civilians, but lending in recompense some useful Danish words (including *give* and *take*, fittingly). With the nation already somewhat harried, in 1066 the piously named King Edward the Confessor died, leaving England in an awkward impasse with no clear heir to the throne. Bickering for the crown ultimately took the form of the Norman Conquest, in which William the Conqueror and an impressive fleet of northern Frenchmen defeated the British in the grippingly bloody Battle of Hastings.

Thus begins the age of Norman England, and Old English begins yet another metamorphosis, becoming (with something of an unimaginative choice of names) Middle English. French words such as *melody* and *strange* begin to trickle through the vernacular, as do more multifarious arrangements of grammar and the letter *Q*. Examining *When the Nightingale Sings* of roundabouts 1310, the Reader may note an increasing familiarity:

When þe nyhtegale singes,
þe wodes waxen grene,
Lef ant gras ant blosme springes
In Aueryl y wene;
Ant love is to myn herte gon
Wiþ one spere so kene
Nyht ant day my blod hit drynkes
Myn herte deþ me tene.

If so inclined, the euphonious Reader may here chant the words aloud, or dramatically perform in modern translation, should this be preferred:

When the nightingale sings,
The trees grow green,
Leaf and grass and blossom springs,
In April, I suppose;
And love has to my heart gone
With a spear so keen,
Night and day my blood it drains
My heart to death it aches.

This represents a tuneful example of Middle English, as well as a terribly depressing lament (and like the letter *thorn*, þ, even the winsome lover's original identity has drifted away with seven hundred years' of abandonment).

French enjoys its aristocratic glory (*gloire*, at the time) days, until the vulgar and popular English twists its way into nobility, law, and literature. Having edged formal French into the Channel among the sea serpents and vagrant fishermen, Middle English does as many nubile young things are wont to do, and experiences a vast, unexpected, unexplained (and possibly uncomfortable) change. In the apparently verbally precarious era of the fifteenth century, people and poets and dukes and dunces begin to articulate vowels less in the sweet and long and sticky bottom of the mouth, and instead higher and shorter towards its ribbed roof. This may have been caused by the mass migrations following the ratty Black Plague, sheer snootiness upon the part of the talkative rich, or (as we suspect) very small and chatty homunculi. Prior to the bookishly revolutionary Shift, when the King spoke of relentless *time*, he would have pronounced it as *teem* (consider now a grandfather clock, swarming with ruby ants), and one who boasted of wearing a *boot* would have sounded to the modern orator as bearing a tattered *boat* upon the left foot. *See* would have been *say*, *house* as *whose* (and whose house is this, pray tell?), before the Shift. The change, one assumes, would have caused a good deal of trouble in the composition of nursery rhymes.

Moreover, the printing press arrives in Britain upon

clacking gothic feet, which spreads bubonic literacy like the aforementioned plague amidst the English speakers, and (exasperatingly) calls for standardized spelling. Appearing as it did in a fairly tumultuous time, it helped to establish the fickle, illogical characters that persist to the vexation of schoolchildren today, such as *though* and *enough, doubt, passion* and *sugar* and *ocean.* Exceedingly exotic and aromatic news of freshly encountered continents is cried over the chapel bells, bringing with it sparkling words such as *moose* out of native North America and Carib *tobacco* with its aromas addictive, the Hindi *calico* and *cummerbund,* the Peruvian *potato* (and its tasty corresponding root).

And, as merchants and the painters of sacred frescoes had long anticipated, there came the dawning of the European Renaissance with many a fanfare of polyphonic philosophy. Very old and decrepit jesters can still recall the revival of Greek and Latin tradition (the pillars, the proportions, the nudes) and their lexicons popping into educated conversation—words such as *drastic, amphibian, fiction* (and from these one can imagine several interesting phrases to be derived). Tracts of eminent sciences, metaphysics, and fantasies bloomed, demanding sundry vocabularies with which to express a new, numinous reality. Thus could Elizabethan physicist William Gilbert (rather proudly, the author admits her ancestral relation) state:

> Peculiar electrical effluvia,
> which   are   the   most
> subtile material of diffuse

humour, entice corpuscles. Electrical effluvia differ greatly from air; and as air is the effluvium of the earth, so electricks have their own effluvia and properties, each of them having by reason of its peculiar effluvia a singular tendency toward unity.

thereby inventing the word *electricity*. (Here, one may also note the simultaneous continuing comprehensibility and sprawling verbosity of Early Modern English.) *Thee, thou*, and the letter *ſ* (a long *S*, ultra-serpentine) were then in *ſtyle*, as were codpieces.

Perhaps the Reader knows, by way of stodgy academy or the limelit unfolding of a theatre's crimson curtains, the reputation of a certain William Shakespeare and his various enduringly popular plays. Famously, or infamously (a most charismatic combination), the man coined words and phrases much in the prolific way that stray cats generate wicked static electricity and kittens. Thus Cordelia of *King Lear* can call for her eponymous father:

All blest secrets,
All you unpublish'd virtues of the earth
Spring with my tears! be aidant and remediate
In the good man's distress! Seek, seek for him;

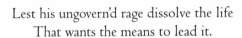

> Lest his ungovern'd rage dissolve the life
> That wants the means to lead it.

This being, according to the Oxford English Dictionary, the earliest use of *unpublished* and *ungoverned* (though *aidant* has fallen out of fashion by now, alas). Shakespeare stands with the fanned collar of a posthumous portrait, credited as well with the invention of *eyeball, noiseless, bedazzle, lustrous* and *lackluster, sanctimonious,* and *fashionable,* and hundreds more (good show, old chap). Nonetheless, one must bear in mind that his works mark only the first documented appearance of such words; one can imagine duchesses and blacksmiths perhaps secretly speaking of *unearthly embraces* (these being attributed to celebrated William) long before the luminous stage of the Globe. Furthermore, some scholar or another is forever maintaining that the playwright himself never existed, and remains solely an artificial ghost whispering lines behind swooning Juliet. Whether or no he lived with true breath, and whether or no he forged such new words out of candlelight and ink, one may still admit the sheer excellence in the mere idea of Shakespearean genius (how proud he might have been, given a singular word of his own), or at least take those soliloquies and swashbuckling dialogues as instances of Early Modern English as spoken by royalty and rabble of the time. Despite the lack of phonographs, tungsten, and bicycles, 'twas an age of innovation, by artful way of tongue and quill.

In these and coming centuries of experiment, poetics,

and pale ships drifting betwixt forbidden latitudes and longitudes and archipelagoes, English unfolds with an ostentatious quantity of words and a somewhat more organized (nevertheless oft-silly) grammar. Various scrawling authors and speculating scientists concoct or assemble or appropriate words of fitting meaning and aesthetics for their own purposes. Alongside the Laws of Motion and several secret elixirs of quicksilver, Isaac Newton finds forces *centrifugal* and *centripetal*. The *phylum* takes form, not purely out of the paralyzed and pearlescent shells of collected beetles, but from biologist Thomas Huxley's adaptation of the Greek (*phyle*, *Φυλή*, a clan or cavalry of ancient Attica). A certain notorious Marquis lends us (with pleasure) *sadism*. Thomas More discovers his self-crafted *utopia* and there articulates an eternal yearning for the nonexistent geography of the immaculate (More coined *absurdity*, too), and John Milton's Eve in her lost paradise tries not to be *loquacious*, while in his *Pamela* Samuel Richardson invents the *fat-face* (ah, brilliance).

Handy scraps of local Gaelic languages cavort their way into English speech, which is why one may describe a home as *cozy* as a cottage in the haunted Scottish moors, inhabited by a *wee* old *fogey*. Irish with its verdure and violins and lilting elegies brings *bards*, bearing news of the *bogs*, telling the tale of a *phony*, singing verses *galore*. And in spite of the fact that the frost-winged, flightless, waddling bird exists nowhere near Wales, still from that language comes *penguin*.

As has proved its historical inclination (a kleptomania

of conversationalists, piracy of chat), English enjoys further thieving and exchanges of words with nearby domains. From France come the pastels and thread of artists' *ateliers*, and the *pianoforte*'s certain plinking *mystique*. *Armadas* of *pimentos*, bearing *machetes* (or vice versa, as the case may be), sail from Portugal and Spain, while out of Holland come the *cabooses* and from Russia the *mammoth*'s mammoth, trumpeting, icebound cry. From Germany we learn how some things (faulty harpsichords, engines operated by cats) go *kaput*, and with rakish smiles the *bandits* come a-riding out of the cypresses of the Italian hills. And Hungary sends horse-drawn *coaches* brimming with *paprika*. Arabic contributes *alfalfa* and *admiral*, and the *ciphers* in the arts of *algebra*.

And of course, in spite of a rather booming, messy, spangled conflict with Britain and its current lunatic king, America retains the English language, but (tectonic drift being an endless natural phenomenon) with many transmogrifications, errors, subtractions, and batty appendages. The attentive Reader might easily discern the audible gulf betwixt the British and Americans in idle chatter (as at times proves necessary in the cinema, in order to discern which archetypical, stereotypical characters are cowboys, gentlefolk, or possibly villains), and furthermore did language become a lively sort of exchange across dominions of seaweed and pilot whales. Words which might be useful upon either continent, such as *scrawny*, *hindsight* (which comes like volcanism to all peoples), *cahoots*, and vaguely coonskin-capped items such as *blizzard*, *bushwhack,* and *rambunctious* enter the vernacular, as did the grand synonyms' chasm between *biscuit* and *cookie.* As brutal Conestoga migrations surge across the American frontier, further native words (and land and lives) are appropriated: the Algonquin *totem* and *raccoon,* the Abenaki *skunk,* the Narragansett *squash.*

    Indeed, with what one may now recognize as a dynamic of fascination, pain, and power without virtue, the richness of the English language links also with the wealth of the European empires, planting flags and colonies every which way it might please. As various peoples and lands and lineages fall under the British Empire's arrogant rule and its lucrative trades, words too are imported into the English throat: in India, enchanted with the tropical image of their own lush *raj,* the British discover Hindi *shampoos* and Urdu *pajamas,* the might of the *typhoon.* Variant sightings of landfall bring Tagalog from the *boondocks* of the Philippines and whorled Tahitian *tattoos.* Criminal (in several senses) colonization of vast Australia begs for the Aboriginal names of leaping *kangaroos* and *wombats* and the bump-nosed *koala,* organisms incomprehensible in their marsupial weirdness, there in the sweltering expanse of what the Europeans could only call the *outback.*

    The imperial fortunes of other nations bring further artifacts of conquered territories, like the dappled shadow of the Guarani *jaguar,* the irresistible *chocolatl* of Nahuatl, the crescent and crunch of Tupi *cashews.* Out of the West Indies and the delphinine Orinoco came the *hurricanes.* And profitable as cruelty can be, the enterprise of American slavery begat an influx of grief and vocabulary, the Angolan *chimpanzees,* Nigerian Ibo *okra, banana* from the Wolof and *gorilla, cola,* and incomprehensible pain for which words do not suffice as an apology. Apart from being a language of poetics regarding daffodils and sublimity and stories of maidens orphaned, this has been the language of those who wield: firearms and flags, power and an endless enthrallment mingled with avarice, a mouth interested in all things at once.

English endures in this the age of flickering screens and insubstantial digital identities—or rather it thrives, tossing its seeds worldwide in nonsensical imports, and reciting a millennia's loot of stolen words, filching more vocabulary from a hundred and operating upon the batty grammatical rules of too many different, ancient tongues. Said Walt Whitman in a most stately way, with leaves of winsome grass caught in his poetical beard: "Viewed freely, the English language is the accretion and growth of every dialect, race, and range of time, and is both the free and compacted composition of all." Or, we might simply conclude, English is a bastard; of course, we mean this in the best possible sense.

'Twas towards the close of the nineteenth century that a number of scholars brought to a zenith their profound interest in just how English came to be just what it happens to be, and how the diligent lexicographer might gather it all into a single tome (see Appendix B, which is rambling somewhere below).

Appendix B:
on the formation of the Oxford English Dictionary and of its paper ancestors, involving geniuses, obsessions amidst the gilt pages, and a murderer

Prior to the nineteenth-century, that era of urgent telegraphs and horse-drawn carriages and the scientific study of the nonexistent ether, English dictionaries had indeed existed. For instance, in 1582 school headmaster Richard Mulcaster, who admirably believed in rigorous education of both females and males and suffered from vague narcolepsy (for *all* history is punctuated, starred by, starry with its oddball characters), composed his *Elementarie*, largely a pedagogical guide for English teachers but notably including a list of eight thousand words and a call for proper spelling. "Forenners and strangers," he chided, "do wonder at us, both for the uncertaintie in our writing, and the inconstancie in our letters." Mulcaster incorporated such forgotten tidbits as *bumbaste* and *flindermouse*, but neglected to provide a definition, which meant that a few fluttering centuries would pass before the words were indicated, respectively, as "to thrash" and "a bat."

In 1604 one Robert Cawdrey published his *Table Alphabeticall* enumerating the spelling and definitions of various popular words, cordially declaring it "gathered for the benefit and help of ladies, gentlewomen, or any other unskillfull persons"; the wise modern Reader

273

can refer to Cawdrey's character—or the philosophy in which he dwelt—as that of a *nincompoop* (a word absent from his *Table*, as it first appears in 1673), but such was the entrenched, fearful, skeletal power of the age. Whilst considered the first true English dictionary (listing *chaos* as "a confused heap or mingle-mangle," which it continues to be), the tome contained but three thousand entries, and one assumes that people from village witches to duchesses, bards and blacksmiths did utilize far more words than that.

Fifty-two years later, Thomas Blount—who dabbled also in hieroglyphics and an "academie of eloquence"—released the *Glossographia, or a Dictionary interpreting all such hard words, of whatsoever language, now used in our refined English tongue, with etymologies, definitions, and historical observations on the same; also the Terms of Divinity, Law, Physick, Mathematicks, and other Arts and Sciences explicated; very useful for all such as desire to understand what they read.* Past its magnificent title, Blount's catalogue of eleven thousand entries neglected not the imports of foreign and vulgar words, nor the interweaving of vivid clarification: to understand *horizon*, "imagine you stood upon Highgate or the Tower-hill at Greenwich, so far as you may see round about, as in a Circle, where the Heaven seems to touch the earth, that is called the Horizon." Blount, one may note, represented a secret teller of tales.

More prominently, a century hence the inimitable polymath Samuel Johnson issued the *Dictionary of the English Language.* Johnson suffered from tics and thrived on translation, drank in doorways, and also authored a fable regarding a Happy Valley of infinitely fulfilled wishes, and moreover he found in English a good deal of "perplexity to be disentangled, and confusion to be regulated." Therefore did he embark upon his own illustrious quest over nine toilsome years, resulting in a highly unwieldy and groundbreaking tome of more than forty-two thousand words and his own didactic throne within the pantheon of linguistic history (which can be a very dusty place). Innovatively, Johnson made partial attempts at etymology, and utilized the quotations of literary luminaries in order to illustrate a word's animation upon the page, though he hesitated not to manipulate the works of his predecessors according to his own predilections. Within his dictionary he remains as an implicit and impertinent jesters' ghost, methodically eliminating those entries he found distasteful, such as *shabby* and *bang*; nonetheless, twenty-three of his words, *loveapple* to *loveknot* to *lovingkindness*, are variations upon metamorphosing *love*. Johnson found, as well, the wry opportunities to insult Scotsmen and the French, and specifies a lexicographer such as himself as "a harmless drudge."

Across the Atlantic—green sea of iceberg, kraken, and excessive metaphor—one Noah Webster, driven by spangled patriotism and the same reform-minded crabbiness which led him to publish a Bible cleansed of its nastier bits which might well seem "especially offensive to females," released his 1828 opus *An American Dictionary of the English Language*. Recognizing the growing diversity between English in the British Isles, fraught with rain and royalty, and the American continent with its unknown golden

West, he proclaimed his grand quest to bring intellect to the nation of rebels and Conestoga trains pressing into a wilderness purportedly their own. Thus did he classify items such as *chowder* in its rustic bowls, while simultaneously campaigning in the easily pronounced name of phonetic spelling, that it might ease *reeding* for *yung* students of the English *tung*. Such efforts did not quite yield the victory for which Webster had hoped.

But in 1857, meeting (one imagines) in a diligently murmuring drove of top hats beneath the iconic rainfall and evocative smog of old London, the earnest bibliophiles of the British Royal Philological Society scrutinized the foibles and holes of previous dictionaries. Their own specially formed Unregistered Words Committee (one of those formidable and invisible titans of vigilante law enforcement, arresting illicit, escapee words in the black of night) revealed a litany of flaws: spotty etymologies, missing connotations, a lack or paucity or dearth or famine of synonyms, and a vast neglect of terms by then considered obsolete, even *nugacious*, or trivial. Thus did the Society raise itself to lexicography's magnificent cause.

A consummate dictionary of the English tongue, it was decided, ought to trace most accurately a word's etymological roots, whether onomatopoeic or ancient as muses, tropical or boreal or unknown. Any dictionary worth the name would link entire families of related words, and include not merely the definition of a word as seemed sensical in modern terms, but the chronicles of its shifting purpose over chattering time.

Genius, for instance, which by the mid-seventeenth century meant a most adept or resourceful, encyclopedic or virtuoso mind, once indicated the guardian ghost of a given place upon the haunted earth, or the attendant spirit guiding for good or ill a person's carnal deeds. A superlative dictionary would seek out its first recorded English usage through the chronogram of a literary quote: as in "O Genius min owne clerke, Come forth and here this mannes shrift," out of the 1390 *Lover's Confession* of John Gower, in which within a forest of verse and sin an overwrought paramour is shown redemption by his own spectral sentinel. A true dictionary ought to illustrate these facts—*for every single word.*

Conceived with the fervency of united scholars—among them the future archbishop of Ireland, and the grandson of opium-mouthed bard Samuel Taylor Coleridge, and one Frederick Furnivall, socialist and ornery autodidact and rather lecherous, amiable leader of a young ladies' rowing club (for recall that like the distortion of space around the brilliancies of wandering stars, all history is constellated by personality)—the epical project of the new dictionary nonetheless waited twenty years to gain in 1879 the sponsorship of Oxford University. Command was passed to James Murray, a Scottish schoolmaster piously free of alcohol and ingeniously self-educated in twenty-five languages of the babbling globe; with that charming humility belonging to some sorts of quiet, earth-toned academia, the vast endeavor was relegated to the Scriptorium, a shed of sagging bookshelves and corrugated iron tucked amid the hushed crocuses of a rear garden. According to the best estimates of the sanguine philologists, one ought to require no more than, eh, ten years to complete the *Oxford English Dictionary*.

Yet given the enormous populace of words murmuring their way across millennial pages and mortal mouths, the present task could be feasibly given not only to a cluster of professorial drones, but begged for a multitude of searchers. Thus, as advertisements beseeched, volunteer readers across the Anglosphere combed texts from the modern to the irrelevant to the crumbling antique. Such willing helpers were instructed to seek not only those most bizarre or obsolete of terms (*okselle*, say, this being the armpit), but indeed the humdrum artifacts of the everyday (*or* and *clock* and *everyday* itself), and to seek out their shifts of meaning and their first known appearance within a cited text. By 1884, more than three million contributions had already arrived on their wax-sealed wings—unfathomably processed and organized through a (likely maddening) system of one thousand and twenty-nine wooden pigeonholes. Yet as of 1894 the *OED* had ascended only as far as *E*, released in serial volumes as if 'twere the arcane comic book of the crusading brainiac.

Literary quotations, marked by their eras' injuries and erroneous sciences and loony protagonists, amounted to a kind of evidence for the virtuous crime of writing in the first place and for the birth of a word. Of those authors making their distinguished appearance amidst the alphabet, Shakespeare with his murky biography and archetypal quill stands as the most-mentioned in the *OED*, though the most frequent coiner of novel neologisms remains seventeenth century Sir Thomas Browne—royal physician of amphibious intellect, he who wrote of the *canicular* howl of the Dog Star and the *Musæum Clausum*, the closed museum of marvels forever lost: a vial of ethereal salt, a ring found in a fish's belly 'neath the course of the good ship *Bucentaur*, and the *quandros*, the noble stone found in a vulture's skull with all the treasures of a scavenger's thoughts (concerning key terms, see the Book at hand, Dear Reader).

As was given to the poetic inconvenience of the nineteenth century, the postal correspondence which made the dictionary had its tactile pleasures, and the inimitable riddles of unknown handwriting and an inky anonymity. As over the years Murray (harried by pronunciation even at his fireside, as the Scriptorium was relocated now to his own yard) inspected the constant and sometimes redundant contributions, he noted especially one particular stream of letters most urbane, immensely erudite, courteous and inscrutable—thousands of definitions and etymologies compiled by an obviously gifted mind with numerous books and a goodly amount of leisure time. The enigmatic Dr. William Chester Minor of Crowthorne, Murray observed, refused all invitations to visit the Scriptorium for a gentlemen's tea.

At last embarking across the chalk hills and muted woods and the drip-drops of white flowerets in southeast England, Murray found himself quite cordially received at a manor of solemn brick and windows barred, relentless walls cloaked in ivy like the lost clothes found beneath the stone cherubs of a cemetery. One can only imagine his slight hesitation, perhaps, as he had now learnt that these were the gardens and locked doors of the Broadmoor Asylum for the Criminally Insane. The studious Mr. Minor—the *poor* Dr. Minor, that one word opening a wound—was a longtime resident and distinguished murderer.

One tries to feel the perplexion of James Murray, confronted with the human wilderness shut within a cell of collected tomes—the very books from which Minor had drawn his researches—facing the indefinable delusion wandering his dictionary. And one must endeavor to know the pleasure of long-imprisoned William Minor, graced with an esteemed guest—just as might anybody in any sophisticated library in the liberated world—tinged with the shame of his acknowledged strangeness, blessed for a moment by an affinity with somebody who dwelt far above his brain's demonic world. Sense now the moment of salutation, its fearful gallantry and the gentle bow.

The decade of lexical work streaming from Crowthorne to the Scriptorium had followed, as Murray learnt, Dr. Minor's own interminable years of paranoia. Upon drooping shoulders, entwined with a wizardly beard, Minor would have carried the vaguely spiced memory of a missionary childhood upon the luniform sweep of Sri Lankan shores, and a Yale education in the mockery of sculpture which was the era's primitive surgery. Still he may have mentioned not his time as a military doctor in

America's Civil War: blood clotting upon the surface of a nameless creek, screams and savagery, the amputated dance of a soldier's shredded leg. But so may be character made and ruptured, the mind snapped.

Minor, one supposes, might have recalled in irredeemable humiliation and febrile lust the lewd streets of New York and London, cobblestones glinting red and reptilian beneath whores' malnourished feet. Of this he would have said nothing to Murray, honorable guest. And never would Dr. Minor have mentioned the smoggy bang and crumpling flesh of that alleyway night when beneath fierce stars he shot a random laborer, and ended in the asylum with little hope of release.

He could have attempted to explain the violence which seemed so logical in a skewed mirror, how the demons slipped through warped floorboards and into his chambers with the tubercular drafts, crawling on nightmare claws across the ceiling and into his perspiring bed, and robbers watched prurient with his beloved belongings in filthy hands. But one must understand the silence of the lunatic—for the world does not mean the same thing for everybody at once.

Yet what inexpressible consolation the dictionary would have brought, what refined conversation and bookish passion might have haloed Minor and Murray as they paced the asylum's grey gardens, a killer's shriek perhaps resounding from a darkened window over the bestial topiaries. What solace must the madman have drawn from the toil and thrill of the dictionary, the taproots of every word linking him to spheres of culture and companionship and a common meaning, however brief the glimpse. We endeavor to comprehend.

And yet after dementia's pathetic poetry, Minor lived not to witness the *Oxford English Dictionary's* completion in 1928 with the heroic release of its last volume; nor did ever-dedicated Murray. One wonders how the two, and Johnson and Cawdrey and sorcerous Thomas Browne moreover all the hundreds of contributors over seventy years of crackling telephones and world warfare and jazz, might have reeled at the ceaseless transmutations and treacheries of English, the constant need for supplements and the thousands of mutant newborn words to add each year. For slang has and continues to giggle its way into relevance, and still people catch the nectary scent of foreign names, while astronomy and oceanography and the quantum flash with their own novel vocabularies, and authors inject terms utterly real in their fiction and suddenly significant in the fantasies of everyday life. No word remains more stable than a chrysalis, frail and iridescent and forever on the webbed verge of metamorphosis or death, meaning taking wing until each book tells a tale entirely different from what it was before—what will happen?

And by now the *Oxford English Dictionary*—from which this book takes its inspirational skeleton—has swollen into nearly one million tragicomic and inconstant and lustrous words. But if its creators and all the aforementioned academia might be called *geniuses* (in the ephemeral parlance of our time), then (the Author wonders) one can name

Minor too, and generations of writers and lunatics and speakers and the still-grandiloquent dead, as possessing geniuses of their own, in the terrifying and spectral sense of centuries past: apparitions perched upon the reader's shoulder and in the crooks of trees, silently touching one's oldest scars, making omens out of animals and logodædaly out of the world. Therefore and in perpetuity, the dictionary is not finished yet.

Erzsébet Gilbert

(ɛəʒbɛt gɪlbɜːt) [Hungarian *Erzsébet*, variant of *Elizabeth*, Greek *Ελισαβετ*, Hebrew *Elisheva*, my god is a promise, and British *Gilbert*, from Old French *Gisil*, noble youth, + *berht*, bright] NOUN

Author of this book.

Daughter of a librarian and an astrophysicist, Erzsébet Gilbert was born in western Colorado in 1984. Following her youth of chimerical stories, willows, and desert stargazing, she graduated from Colorado State University having studied Creative Writing and the History & Philosophy of Science. Concurrent with writing, schooling, and the creation of this book, Gilbert has traveled to some forty countries, including six Mediterranean months spent living in a Volkswagen bus, a trans-Siberian railway pilgrimage to glimpse a total solar eclipse, and journeys amidst the bougainvillea of Southeast Asia. She and her spouse, author David Rozgonyi, now live beside a castle wall in southwest Hungary, where she keeps a working vineyard and is presently at work on a novel regarding love, grief, and the history of astronomy.

Sherise Talbott

(ʃəɜːis tælbɒt) [English variant of French *Cerise, Cherise,* cherry, and Norman French *Talbert,* from Old French *Talbod,* from *tal,* wartime, + *bod,* tidings, a messenger] NOUN

Illustrator of this book.

Sherise Talbott has always been charmed by imaginative worlds and magical creatures. She grew up in Colorado around the Rocky Mountains, inspired by nature and the evergreen forests. She spent time creating journals and drawing her fantasies into the pages. It wasn't until her adulthood that she started to take her creativity seriously. Her education is in Fine Arts, focusing on Ceramics. She is a self-taught Illustrator, and spends many of her days dreaming up stories and poems for children and adults. Currently she resides in Denver, Colorado, where she dreams of travelling to faraway lands. She has lived in Finland and New Zealand; she's spent some time in South America, learning about the jungle and exploring the coast. She is currently working on a children's book and aspires to continue working in her studio, throwing pottery and illustrating her imagination.